Twilight of Eclipse and Eternity

Michael Neno

Copyright @2021 by Michael Neno

All rights reserved. No part of this book may be reproduced in any form or by any electronic or mechanical means, including information storage and retrieval systems, without permission in writing from the publisher, except by reviewers, who may quote brief passages in a review.

This publication contains the opinions and ideas of its author. It is intended to provide helpful and informative material on the subjects addressed in the publication. The author and publisher specifically disclaim all responsibility for any liability, loss or risk, personal or otherwise, which is incurred as a consequence, directly or indirectly, of the use and application of any of the contents of this book.

WORKBOOK PRESS LLC
187 E Warm Springs Rd,
Suite B285, Las Vegas, NV 89119, USA

Website:	https://workbookpress.com/
Hotline:	1-888-818-4856
Email:	admin@workbookpress.com

Ordering Information:
Quantity sales. Special discounts are available on quantity purchases by corporations, associations, and others.
For details, contact the publisherfl at the address above.

You may also contact the author at pstinson23@comcast.net or http://gogoreadgo.blogspot.com phone # 1-763-788-3042

Library of Congress Control Number:
ISBN-13:   978-1-955459-78-5 (Paperback Version)
            978-1-955459-79-2 (Digital Version)

REV. DATE: 09/06/2021

TWILIGHT OF
ECLIPSE AND ETERNITY

By: Michael Neno

Acknowledgement

This is a way of acknowledging those who have helped me along the way.

To my loving wife Michelle, I owe you a lot since the beginning until now.

To my family and friends, you've been a big help.

Telling my story has allowed me to reflect on how far I've come to inspire more people to look always at the brighter side of life.

And also the fact that I have been supported by the very best, to whom I can only say a truly heartfelt thank you.

INTRODUCTION

There are special times in time and space where it is possible to let your love concur the barriers between life and death to reunite the two parts of a love that has been untimely torn apart.

It happened for me and Jane, the woman that I had loved ever since we first met as teenagers at school and started dating twelve years previously. These times only become apparent on certain days when the cosmic forces are willing to open themselves up and to let the spirit of a person whose soul is crying out for their loved one to pass from beyond the veil of death to visit their soul mate for a short while or be reunited.

It had been four months since the woman I loved died in a car accident while returning home after seeing some friends on the 11th of August in the year of 1998. After spending the rest of that year shut away from the world around me in my sadness over the one that I lost I was finally going to see in the beginning of the new year of 1999 by joining the huge crowds of revellers and remember the one I loved and lost so tragically some time before.

CHAPTER 1

We first met when Jane joined my school in the town of Newton Priory after she and her family moved into my area of Devon where I lived from another part of the country. She was athletically slim with flowing wavy blonde hair and blue eyes, funny, caring; smart and all the things that guys dream their girl would be like. After being placed in the same class as I attended she quickly became the centre of attention to the other lads in it including myself; but not being particularly brainy, sporting or good looking I settled for just being there.

All through the final two years of school I considered myself right out of her league as she was never without a boyfriend be he the captain of the school soccer team or from a well off family financially and there I was not good enough for sport and from a family that was struggling just to make ends meet. Unknown to me at the time events were falling into place that would change things forever for both of us.

It all began when Jane was starting to be pressured by her boyfriend to go all the way sexually with him which she never wanted to so he began getting aggressive with her, with his popularity as a school sporting captain dismissing his behaviour. It was a Friday evening at the local youth club that things came to a head with them and I found myself drawn into their troubles. After drinking some alcohol which he had sneaked into the club Jane's boyfriend grabbed her arm and with her calling out for help amid the loud music being played dragged her into a small store room adjacent to the main hall as nobody took any notice believing it to be playing around.

At first I tried to ignore it, which was until I saw the tears that were running down Jane's face and the look of fear in her eyes which was when I knew that I had to do something about it. The screams saying "Leave me alone, get off me, I don't want to have sex with you." So taking a deep breath I followed them into the still darkened store room where the struggling by her to get free had already knocked some things off of some shelving and found the lad pulling and tearing at her cloths. Grabbing him by his shoulder I pulled him off her punching hard hitting him in the face with a well-placed right hook causing his nose to start bleeding. On hearing the noise several other guys came in and as I called out "He's raping her get him off." they forcefully removing him from the premises leaving me to place my jacket over her shoulders to hide her ripped top. The police were called and after only a matter of minutes they arrived arresting her boyfriend. After her very upsetting experience I found myself being the only one to comfort her. That night I walked her home and for the first time since she had joined my school and we talked enabling us to find an unexpected friendship.

The phones must have been busy that weekend because by the Monday morning the whole school was full of talk about the way that I had been a hero by saving Jane from her wicked boyfriend who had tried to rape her and how she had dumped him for me. She had dumped him that was true but we were not going out together. In the morning supported by Jane dressed in her school uniform an officer from the police and the school principle talked to the students about what had happened on the Friday night. Mr Smedley the principle announced the inclusion of an after school self-defence class which Jane was the first to enrol on. He also told everyone that her ex had been expelled and had been charged with sexual assault. And all that was until a couple of weeks later when after spending almost all of her time with me I plucked up the courage to ask her out.

It was whilst we were sitting in the school restaurant having a hot coffee after eating that I took hold of her hand across the table and said, "I know I've got nothing to offer a girl like you but will you go out with me?" "You've got more than you know to offer any girl and yes I will." Came her reply. That was enough for me but for the many sets of eyes that were scrutinising us it wasn't, so Jane I think conscious of them leant across the table and kissed me fully on the lips causing my lips to tingle like they had electricity flowing through them. For her that was enough to let everyone know that I was now her guy and by the end of the day everybody knew it. "My parents know what you did to save me and I want to take you home so that they can meet and thank you." She said to me which I bashfully accepted.

During the final three months of our schooling the two of us were almost inseparable spending barely any time apart in school or out of it. On the most part we studied for our exams together but we did still found the time to kiss and cuddle whenever away from prying eyes mainly in a quiet corner of the school library and after school in the back row of the local cinema. The routine of studying Monday until Friday followed by going to the cinema or to a party on Saturday night was how things went for us until the end of our final exams and leaving school to join the world of finding work.

Going out into the grown up world and finding work although time consuming came relatively easy to us both. Jane having a perfect shape as a model and l a position as a sales assistant in a large local retail supermarket. During the week Jane would be travelling around the country with her modelling while I was kept busy filling the shelves with goods for the store customers to purchase, but at weekends anyone could find us together. I found it incredible how a beautiful girl like Jane would wish to be with me but all the same just being with her made me feel special.

It was with Jane's prompting that on my seventeenth birthday I placed a deposit down on a 100cc motorbike with the money which I had saved over the previous ten months from my wages the intention being to ride that for a year to get a good road sense and then to buy and learn to drive a car. Another thing that happened on my birthday was the two of us became engaged making plans to get a small place of our own. Everything for me felt like I was actually living a dream, a dream so perfect in every way that I often expected to wake up but I didn't.

During the rest of March, all of April and the start of May Jane and I spent as much time as possible viewing properties for sale trying to find that special place to be our first home together. It was on Saturday May the eight 1997 that the two of us viewed a small one-bedroom flat, built on the ground floor of Victorian brick building and being located on the outskirts of the local town fell in love with it quickly putting in an offer to buy it which was accepted and seven weeks later we were able to move in.

On the fourth of July a Saturday we were given the keys to our new home and started to move our processions in. We spent the day unpacking our belongings and arranging the small amount of furniture which we had accumulated beforehand before settling down to spend our first night together. Because we had been so busy during the day with unpacking I nipped out and returned with a Chinese takeaway for our evening meal. It wasn't in any way that special but the bottle of cheap wine, soft music and a bunch of red roses made it quite romantic for us. Later Jane and I snuggled up on our couch to watch a video on the T.V and she moved herself closer and closer to me letting me know in my heart that I was the one she wanted to be with. Everything was feeling so good and right when suddenly she jumped up and rushed out of the room. "What's up, what are you doing love." I called out only to have her return moments later with a letter which she had written for me. Sitting back down beside me she said,

Through good times and bad.

My friend, my buddy, Through happy and sad.

Beside me you stand, Beside me you walk,

You're there to listen, You're there to talk,

With happiness with smiles With pain and tears,

I know you'll be there, throughout the years.

When you want to ask the answer is YES. I love you now and always will.

I knew these were words written by another person's hand but the feeling inside of me became feelings of joy and contentment and so I took a hold of Jane's hand I reached into my trouser pocket and pulled out the engagement ring that I purchased a few weeks earlier saying, "I know that we are still too young to wed yet but in my heart I know that you are my one true love, so Will you marry me when we're eighteen.?" Putting her hands around my neck she pulled me toward her and kissed me saying, "You are my love, my destiny and my future. YES, I will marry you. Now I must try to carry on without her. This was hard for me as almost every day I would see or hear something and think, "Ah Jane will like that," I had to keep reminding myself that she was dead and try to get over her, but in my heart I still felt close to her. Every night I had nightmares about that terrible night when she was taken ever so suddenly from my side.

It was on the 10th of August 1998 when she kissed me after returning home from a model friend's house saying, "We're now both eighteen so let's book our wedding." These were words which I myself had been longing to say, so I without hesitation said, "We can do it next weekend my love" That was enough to bring a few tears of joy to her eyes as we got to our feet and we retired to our new bedroom to make love before settling down to sleep. While recovering from several hours of love making Jane looked at me and said, "As soon as we get married I want us to have a baby." I couldn't think of anything better to say other than, "Well stop taking your pill and let's start our family." Well what can I say other than we didn't sleep much that night or come to think of it we didn't sleep that much for a long time after that. On waking up the following morning I looked down at this beautiful woman in my arms and decided there and then that I would rather chew off my arm than wake her up. After the two of us had fully woken and got out of bed, dressed and eaten some breakfast Jane told me that she wanted us to visit her friend so that she could show off her diamond engagement ring to her that night to which I agreed. That was to be the last day we would be together. By the morning Jane would be dead, killed tragically in a car accident. I think a large part of me died along with her on that dark narrow country lane in the pouring rain. Even months later I found myself continuing to have flashbacks to that day, that is until my experience while at her graveside.

CHAPTER 2

With the memory of Jane was still so clear in my mind I promised myself to be at her grave side on the stroke of midnight to pray for her spirit. So at fifteen minutes before midnight I put down my drink departing from the party which I had made myself attend, setting off in the fresh cold damp air and set about walking through the thick mist that hung in the air toward the church where she had been buried four months earlier. Even then I was aware of a strong feeling of needing to be at her graveside on that night within me as if I was being called to attend.

As I made my way along the quiet and relatively empty streets towards the church with my left hand holding my jacket collar close around my neck for warmth and my right hand holding a single red rose to place on her grave my thoughts were of Jane and the happy times we had shared together. I walked along the loose gravel pathway and into the graveyard at ten minutes to midnight past the 13th century granite built church and made my way along the footpath with the crunching sound from the gravel beneath my feet towards the small willow tree which stood over Jane's grave sheltering it from the elements so as to be as close to her as I could be on this night of all nights.

As I knelt down beside the last resting place of the woman I loved my thoughts were taken back to that night some months before when Jane and I had still been together and looking forward to a long and happy life together as a husband and wife. I can't explain what happened to me there but as I reminisced over the years that I was with her and that fateful night I'm sure that out of the silence in the graveyard I heard her soft voice calling to me from out of the mist. "Mike my love I'm here with you. We can be together again"

Straight away I jumped back to my feet looking around me for her but she wasn't there. Thinking that I had just imagined it in my subconscious mind I placed the rose which I had taken with me onto the top of her grave and with a tear in my eye and a heavy heart said

"I'm never going to forget you my love." As the time reached midnight and the church bells started ringing out the end of the last year and new one in I could easily hear the sound of cheers and celebrations raising up from every direction as the world welcomed in the beginning of a new year and I wished that the one I loved was there to share it with me. my mind filled with thoughts of my Jane and lost all those months ago I could feel my heart seeming to cry out for the chance to be with her again and try to change what had happened. The trauma of what had happened was so great that I seriously considered killing myself to be with her but I did know that we would still be apart if I did.

Suddenly as if in answer to my hopes and prayers I found myself sitting back in the car next to Jane driving back along that same narrow country road as if time itself had been halted and turned back four months. She was in a joyful mood tipsy after being hired to model a mew range of women's summer dresses and wearing one of the new outfits home, a thigh length tight black dress that showed all of her curves. But why was I there of all places was I going to be put through that same terrifying accident, or could I in some way manage to stop it from happening in that I did not know. All I knew was going around the sharp bend in the road that lay only seconds away we would be struck by a farm tractor reversing out of a field gateway and the car that we were in would be crumpled up and burst into flames ending the life of my one true love. Without even thinking about it I shouted out to Jane, "Stop! Quick Stop!" Jane pushed down on the brake pedal but the car carried on. We never stopped in time and just like four months previously as we rounded the bend in the road we struck the rear of the trailer attached to the tractor. The front end of our car folded in on itself pushing the steering column into Jane's chest making her cry out in agonising pain. I was catapulted through the windscreen and onto the twisted mass that was the front bonnet of the car in time to feel the heat of the fire that had ignited inside the engine compartment. Clambering off the mass of twisted metal that was her car I made straight for the driver's door to get Jane out only to be met by horror.

In the driver's seat was Jane her soft smooth skin hanging off her face burning. "JANE!!! Why must I go through all this again?" As I sank to the ground in pain and tears wanting answers as to why this could happen and why wasn't it me there instead of her. But this was happening again what I knew was a dead Jane turned and faced me asking, "How much do you love me Mike?" and then just like time had returned to normal I was back in the graveyard beside her grave standing there in total silence and disbelief.

I could no-longer feel the cold air or the dampness of the mist on my face, it was like everything had paused around me and then it happened. Out of the mist appeared the figure of a beautiful young woman walking toward me with her arms held out in front of her and I recognised Jane just as I remembered her.

She was wearing a long pure white satin dress with her long curly blonde hair flowing in the breeze, beautiful giving a display. Getting home again about 2am I was surprised when I walked into my front door by the sound of movement coming from my Kitchen. There was somebody in my home, but all of my doors and windows had been closed and locked by me on going out. I tip toed into my living room thinking that I had got an intruder and feeling around for something to protect myself with. My right hand touched onto a cricket bat leaning against the hallway wall so I grabbed hold of it and moved as quietly as possible in the direction of my Kitchen intent on bashing my intruder with it.

As I crept into the Kitchen with my cricket bat at the ready I almost collapsed when standing before me I saw Jane. "What, what, what, what are you doing here!" I stammered in total shock and with quivering legs. "How did you get here? Why are you here?" were questions that I managed to get out before she stepped toward me opening her mouth to speak. "I'm here for you my love. No-one else can see or hear me." All I knew was that for a four whole months I'd not lived because when she had died in that mass of bent and twisted car wreckage I had also died inside.

With so much time being apart from her I wanted to take her into my arms and hold her again as I had done so many times in the past. Moving toward her I put my arms up ready to hold and kiss her but as I did so my hands just passed through her just as if she wasn't there. "We can't make physical contact yet Mike. We have to wait a while but soon we will be able to" she said as my eyes looked at her as though searching for answers. For the rest of the night Jane stood as I sat just talking until about 7 am when she said, "Mike. I've got to go. I have to go now because if I don't I will never be able to come back to you." With that she made a kiss to me with her lips and faded away.

To see Jane just fade away to nothing before my very eyes was hurting equally as bad as watching her coffin lowered into the ground some months earlier and as with then I was soon in tears. My only consolation was in her words where she said that she would be back and with time the two of us could be together again. There was just one question going through my head that I was admittedly worried about Lindsey, a dark haired beautiful looking girl who had been Jane's best friend in life and had been a fellow model often working together had just arrived at the front door. She could instantly tell that I was troubled by something so I invited her in so as to talk about the previous night's happenings.

As I related the previous night's happenings to her she seemed to already be fully aware of it as she too had a similar experience as I did. She told me how she had seen Jane in a dream and had been told how I could be reunited with her in time. I'm not a believer in the paranormal as a rule but I am open-minded to the possibility. So there was Lindsey and I pondering how Jane could come back from the dead months after she had died.

The two of us spent the rest of the day together reminiscing over the years that along with Jane we had shared which were full of fun and games together until late into the night. At exactly 11.55pm the same time as the crash that killed her we felt a sudden chill of cold air as our nostrils filled with the scent of Jane's favourite perfume and the large mirror that hung on my wall started reflecting an image of her sitting on the couch beside us. Lindsey jumped up and I just froze where I was sat but not in fright but more in apprehension of who knew what. There was no-one there but the mirror still showed Jane sitting beside us. Could this be a trick of the light or maybe I was seeing her in my subconscious mind I couldn't say but one thing that made it real for me was Lindsey could see exactly the same thing as I could. "What's going on Mike? Is Jane a ghost now? If she is I'm not frightened." For the next ten minutes we just sat there as if glued to our seats and watched the reflection of Jane as it smiled back at us moving her lips as if talking. After some minutes the reflection of Jane faded away leaving Lindsey and I feeling totally at ease and for myself in particular I was feeling a certain excitement at the chance of getting her back and asking myself what I had to do to help her return to me.

Although neither of us spoke to others about this over the course of the next few months I found myself drawn into a routine of having visitations from the spirit of Jane every night appearing in my wall mirror at 11.55pm triggered off by the aroma of her perfume in the air around me. On a lot of these nights Lindsey was with me so knew that I was not going mad or having a mental breakdown in my sorrow. But with all this we were getting frustrated by not being able to talk to or hear her as she seemed to try communicating with us. This was upsetting for me as I could plainly see in Jane's face that she wanted to talk to me as she had done when first appearing to me in the graveyard the first time. Things carried on much the same into March when on the night before my birthday something happened which both surprised me and made me happy in a way that I hadn't been in such a long time.

It was as I said the night before my birthday and Lindsey had come around with a card and a bottle of wine to try and get me to celebrate this special day. I honestly never felt like it without the woman who I loved to share it with, but she managed to persuade me into having a glass with her which I did appreciate. One glass quickly led into another glass and that turned into another and another so by 11.55pm when Jane's image appeared in the mirror I was quite tipsy from the wine and Lindsey who was pouring it was like wise just as inebriated as I was. "I've done what you asked me to do in my sleep last night Jane" said Lindsey trying to look sober as she and it was the amount of drink that I had consumed but I believe Jane spoke to me saying, "It won't be long until we can be together now babe. Happy birthday my love. I love you more than you'll ever know" before fading away this time into Lindsey as though the two of them were joining together. The arrival of morning found both Lindsey and I asleep huddled up on the lounge floor almost naked with both of us hung over from the previous night's drinking. I was the first to wake and on seeing our positions I hurriedly rushed into my bedroom and quickly dressed while being aware of Lindsey.

"What happened last night I was out of it." was the first thing asked by Lindsey on waking and finding herself curled on the floor still half naked but I was finding it difficult to remember much myself. I could however recollect some of what had happened and I was struggling to make sense out of it in my head asking myself if I had imagined it or if it did indeed happen as I thought it had. One thing that did weigh heavily on my conscience was the good feeling which I was getting having from this lovely young lady on my floor, something that I hadn't experienced since that dreadful night so many months earlier.

As I struggled to remember the night before I had one question and that was whether her spirit was still inside Lindsey and why would she choose to do such a thing to me as in letting me make love to her best friend's body.

Closing my eyes still half asleep, I had let my mind wonder back to the many occasions when I was in the same position with Jane, but having felt Lindsey's warm body next to mine I couldn't help but kiss her fully on the lips saying, " I love you Jane with all my heart." Before I had even opened my eyes again and returned to the present Lindsey put a hand up to my face and kissed me back with the same love as Jane had and very quickly things became intimate as I made love with Jane through Lindsey's body, but she was gone again and I had just been unfaithful without knowing or intending to.

After what had just happened I felt as though I had done something very bad by betraying Jane with her best friend but that wasn't the all of it. As I lay face down on the floor afraid to move or even face Lindsey she stood up, stepped forward facing the mirror and said in a warm soft voice, "I'm so sorry Jane I felt it all last night as well. Now I know why you want to come back so bad." As I lay there engrossed by Lindsey's actions it quickly transpired that somehow Jane's spirit had merged with Lindsey's body enabling her to make physical contact with me. This happening put my mind at ease to a certain extent, but it did cause me considerable worry as Lindsey had herself experienced the whole thing meaning that I had made love with her as well as with Jane and that was to me being unfaithful. The only consolation to me was to once again make love with Jane but I had to via having sex with Lindsey.

Right through the rest of March, all of April and most of May neither Lindsey nor I spoke of what had transpired on my birthday but we both knew that something had happened between us. I could tell that affection had grown within her for me and I would be a liar if I tried to say that she still held no appeal to me. Fortunately for me my love for Jane overcame the temptation to get that close to Lindsey again as they were like sisters before the accident anyway.

CHAPTER 3

Meanwhile, with all of the things which were occupying my head I was unaware of the things that had taken a hold in Lindsey's mind. I was ignoring her and her feelings and was without realising it denying her the opportunity of expressing herself to me. I failed to even notice the way that after the night of my birthday in March she had started spending almost every day that she was not away working with me be it going out for a drink or just sitting in front of the television set and talking.

To most people who knew us the generally accepted thought was that I had finally moved on with my life by getting over my loss of Jane and was now dating her best friend. That in truth was not the case but under different circumstances I would of been very happy if it was. Neither of us was particularly concerned about what others thought. No-body knew or would understand the things that had happened. To be honest I don't think that Lindsey or I really understood but we were happy with the idea of seeing my love and her best friend again.

It was the end of May when I was dropped a bombshell by Lindsey. After having spent so many evenings together waiting and hoping for contact from Jane's spirit to inform us of when and how she could return to life she confessed to loving me, This was not the thing that I wanted to hear as I myself was becoming confused inside about my feeling for her. Yes, she was my loves best friend and yes as such she had become a good friend to me, but my love was dead and Lindsey was a beautiful young woman plus we had already been intimate with each other be it in the guise of Jane's spirit using her body to join with me in the act of love. I was starting to ask myself if I should try and forget Jane and get together with Lindsey, but each time I found myself questioning my own feelings I remembered that night in the graveyard and the words of my loves spirit.

That night burdened with confusion and doubt I went out for a walk finding myself drawn without realising it to the grave of Jane where in the cool air of spring I prayed for help in my predicament. As if in response to my prayers like several times already I found myself back in her car sitting next to Jane driving toward the inevitable crash that had taken her away from me all those months earlier.

Unlike the other times I just sat there quietly and accepted the inevitable outcome of what was to follow, but this time there was a noticeable difference. As we approached the bend in the road where we were going to crash Jane looked over at me and said something quite new. She told me in her soft voice, "It's almost the time my darling keeps your faith in me and don't worry about what is going to happen. I love you." With that we rounded the bend and smashed head on into the tractor trailer. As I felt myself being thrown through the windscreen I found myself suddenly back in the graveyard.

It was on the morning of the first Sunday of June 1999 the 6th that a knock on my front door signalled the time that was to test my trust and faith in a woman who was no more. Opening the door, I was greeted by two large policemen who straight away said, "We are here to ask you to accompany us to the police station and answer some questions concerning the desecration of the grave of Miss Jane Thompson." "What do you mean? What's happened?" was my stunned reply. "It appears that last night person or person's unknown exhumed the body of Miss Thompson and we want to ask you some questions about it." was the explanation from the taller of the two officers stood before me.

Within only a couple of seconds I had grabbed my leather motorbike jacket and was in the back of a police car being driven to the station where there was a CID officer awaiting me to talk about what had happened. Still unsure of what had happened or why I had been taken to the police station I was getting quite concerned. I was shown into a small cell like interview room quickly being joined by the CID officer who from first appearance looked rather nerve-racking. I can plainly remember the feeling of unease at not knowing why I was there, but very soon I would know and all would become clear.

After introducing himself as DC Ammet a big built dark haired man with a look that could unsettle even a hardened criminal sat down at the desk where I was sitting and preceded to ask me questions about the previous night's happenings. It soon transpired that at some point during the previous night Jane's body had been dug up and now all that remained was an empty grave with an empty coffin laid in the bottom of it. What I was not told is her body had been dug up from the inside out. Had I have been told that then I would have known that somehow Jane had got herself out which in itself was amazing as she was definitely dead the year before.

"I know it was you. You were seen there by someone. Where is the body? What have you done to it? Why did you do it?" was the first of many questions. Yes, I had been by her grave that night but I hadn't dug it up. I relayed it to DC Ammet who I doubt believed me. Hearing this news upset me greatly which I think the officer picked up on and he left the room leaving me in my sorrow. Once alone I cupped my face in my hands and broke down in tears. I was asking myself why someone would do such a horrible thing as dig up the body of a dead person and then I remembered. I remembered the words of Jane's spirit in that I should keep my faith in her and not worry about what was going to happen. Suddenly as if all the sorrow and worry was being swept away from me I began feeling as though everything would become clear.

On returning DC Ammet informed me that the forensics people had managed to find a very small amount of testable material by the grave which would enable them to get a DNA sample and until they had the results I would be kept in custody. He finished off by telling me that an officer would be bringing me a drink and something to eat a bit later and departed. All I could do was sit back and wait for the forensic results to come back.

Although I was understandably worried as to what was going to happen I knew that I had not done anything wrong or bad, and time would show just that, but all the same there was a part of me still worried that Jane's body had been dug up for some sort of bad reason. Within the hour I was brought a cup of tea and taken to a cell where I would have to spend the night. As I slept in my cell which was about eight feet by six that night my dreams were full of Jane and the time we had spent together before her death. It came as a great surprise to me when at 11.55 pm my cell filled with a bright white light and the image of Jane appeared from out of the wall and approach me as I looked over at her. In her soft voice she softly said, "I know you're scared that you are going to get into trouble for digging me up but there's nothing to be worried about, I had to be free from my coffin so I can come back to you." All that I could do was cry until she continued with, "When the full eclipse comes make sure you're at the place where I died and I'll be back." with that she appeared to turn and walk back through the wall just below the 12-inch bared window above the bench that I was sitting on.

It was at 9.30am the following morning that DC Ammet entered the cell and said, "Will you tell me what the hell is going on with you and this Jane Thompson because I'm stuck here trying to solve a crime that can't be explained." I looked up into his stern face and asked what he meant by what he said. Sitting down beside me the officer opened a file which he was carrying taking out the forensic report relating to the tests carried out on the material that were found at the graveside the day before, This report showed that she was pregnant but that she had only just conceived. She couldn't have known that she was. As it was, it was mine and my pain instantly doubled.

Sliding the file back across the table top toward the officer he said, "There is no reason for you to be kept in custody for now, but if I find out that you're involved in all this in any way I'll come down on you like a ton of bricks! You are free to go but I would like you to look at this in case you can help us" I picked up and opened the report and quickly discovered that the fresh material discovered at the graveside was from a spot of blood found on the outside of the coffin lid. A fresh spot of Jane's blood had been found. Finding this out though not that surprising was still a shock to me as almost a year after the accident that killed her evidence had been found proving she was alive only 24 hours earlier." Can I talk off the record to you Michael?" followed a nervous request from DC Ammet looking almost afraid to ask. "Yes sir anything to help go ahead" was my reply to which he thanked me and then started to share his suspicions with me. Thompson is still alive but I'm at a lost to explain it because the girl that died in an accident last year was positively identified as her. How can a person that was confirmed dead be alive now almost a year later?" Pausing for a few seconds before continuing with," I get the feeling that there is something unnatural or supernatural going on here and I'm at a lost to explain it" to finish off his statement he said, "I've checked you out so I know about the connection you have to this girl and I want to understand what's happening." I related to DC Ammet what I knew as he sat transfixed to my words everything which had happened during the previous months before leaving the cell that I was in and leaving the police station to return home.

As I walked out of the doors and into the bright sunlit day I suddenly found myself inundated with question by news reporters concerning what had happened to Jane and accusations of body stealing for sick reasons and cry s of lock him up and kill him from others. Pushing my way through the hoard of people I felt a sense of not being alone. My heart started beating faster as although I couldn't see or hear anything, I was very much aware of not being alone. Jane or should I say the spirit of Jane was right there beside me. "I told you not to worry my love. Soon we can be together and we will never be parted again." echoed her soft voice from out of nowhere. "Did you know that you were pregnant?" I said feeling incredibly proud and happy inside but saddened more by my double loss." I know Mike and our daughter can't wait to meet you. It's very important that you do what I ask you to do when asked." came her reply to me before seeming to go again. She knew that she was pregnant and it was going to be a little girl but how could anyone have known unless in death she found out.

Walking into the parking area outside I was met by Lindsey looking every bit the beautiful model radiating joy and relief at my coming out free, smiling with an obvious excitement at the news she undoubtedly was eager to share with me, we threw our arms around each other and hugged. Even before we had finished hugging she said with an air of excitement coupled with a little disbelief, "She's back isn't she?" to which all I could do was say, "I think so. Her grave is empty and tests have proved she was there alive yesterday only 24 hours ago." She went on to say, "I've got to tell you something babe. It's important!"

she went on to proclaim, so I suggested going back to my place so that we could have a drink and talk more.

As Lindsey and I started to walk along the pathway which ledd There's more to all this than you're telling me. I'm not after your blood here. I want to understand what's going on and I want to help if I can. I'm not talking as a police officer here so doesn't think of me as one. OK. Call me John. I'm talking asd to speak. Now it was time for Lindsey to tell me what had happened with her earlier while I was still in the police cell. "It was this morning when I was going into town to do some shopping. I was about to go and try on a new dress to wear out for a party when I'm sure I saw Jane looking at some lingerie in the the next isle. When I looked over at her she turned and looked straight back at me and lifted her finger to her mouth as if to say quiet. It surprised me so much I dropped everything and left the shop. I saw her again in the ladies when I was freshening up about half an hour later and she spoke to me." "What did she say?" I asked with excitement before she continued with "She just said to get ready for the eclipse and have faith and trust her." The forecast eclipse! I had been so engrossed with Jane and having contact with her spirit I had completely forgotten about it.

Looking at my watch I saw it was the 13th of June now meaning that the first incident at Jane's grave had been two months before the date of the coming eclipse, but to be honest I couldn't understand what the eclipse had to do with her returning from the dead. "If you've seen her Lindsey then surely we have to find her now for me." I said almost in desperation. "No! It's not time Mike. The time isn't right yet for you." came her reply which made me go quiet. "If anyone does it wrong the passage way between you two will be broken and she'll never be able to come back. Not even her spirit and you'll need to find someone else to love. That much I do know" came her somewhat warning. "There is one private thing between us that I have to tell you later but it can wait for now."

While Lindsey and I shared her news with him John just sat patiently listening in awe with his mouth open at what he was hearing for a short while before finding the words to ask a question. "So if you don't mind my asking. What are you going to do now?" he asked totally wrapped in what he had heard. "What can we do?" I said, "It's obvious that I can't do anything until August the eleventh and the eclipse. I just wish I knew what." I answered.

It was John who came up with an idea, that being to check the security camera's coverage of the shop where Jane had been seen by Lindsey and have me make a positive identification of her just to confirm it was her and not a lookalike playing some sort of cruel joke on me. I agreed because I wanted to see Jane probably more than anyone.

Within the hour I was sitting with John watching the shops security camera footage looking for the appearance of Jane. "There's Lindsey just entered" said John as we saw her entering the shop and walking along the main aisle towards the dresses, but I couldn't see Jane. We watched our eyes fixed to the action as she worked her way through the dresses taking some and holding them up against her and then putting them back. "So where is she?" asked John as we looked for her, but he saw nothing. For a good half of an hour we were glued to the monitor, and then it happened. Lindsey had picked out one dress and was holding it up to her when we saw her suddenly look over towards the lingerie section where she had claimed to have seen Jane. We watched as she dropped the dress that she had been looking at on the floor and rushed over to the lingerie almost running before stopping dead in her tracks. She then appeared to be talking to someone for a few seconds before turning to rush out of the store. What we couldn't understand was the way that on screen there was nobody there which had us both confused. How could Lindsey have seen and spoken to Jane in a store where the security camera only filmed her. What we hadn't realized or saw was in the mirror on the wall used by customers trying new cloths against them was an image of Jane while in front of it was nothing.

We walked out of the store disappointed by what we had or hadn't seen into the rain which had started while there. Looking up and down along the street we could see the public rushing from store to store as they were trying to avoid getting too wet from the heavy shower that had started as we ourselves walked fast to get back to my place where we could dry off and have a hot drink neither of us sure of what was going on.

CHAPTER 4

"Well it's time for me to get back on the job, so I'll leave you to it. But do you mind if I keep up to speed on what's going on here as a friend. Not as a police officer." asked John reassuringly as he stood up from the armchair where he had been sitting. "Yeah John if you want to. But I'm not sure that I know what's going on here now. All I know is something is happening that I have no control over." As he walked out of my front door I turned to look at Lindsey as she sat there with a complete blank expression on her face and a look of bewilderment in her eyes. More so I saw a sign of fear owing to the presents of TV news reporters who had gathered outside wanting a story and answers to why Janes grave had been opened and her body stolen. One reporter aiming his question at John asked if I was being charged for what had appeared to of happened to which without answering he made sure that he could be seen shaking my hand and thanked me for my help with the police investigation. As he was leaving John said within earshot of the press, "I'll let you know if we find out anything. Thank you again." Being heard saying that told the them that I was not a suspect or involved and the waiting press slowly dispersed.

That sorted out I closed my door and returned to Lindsey who was quite upset at the in tine I said, "I know all this must have you so confused and scared but I do believe what you have said. I know there are things going on that nobody can explain, but we must have faith and allow ourselves to follow Jane's directions. Remember she was your best friend as well as my love." Saying that Lindsey's eyes filled with tears as she replied with a shock and unexpected statement. "I know Jane is always going to be the one you love, and she was my best friend almost like a sister but." She paused for about a minute before taking a deep breath and continuing with, "I am in love with you Mike and want you to make love to me without her in me like that night when I let Jane use my body to make love with you. All I want is to have you for my own" Those few words should of been enough to set my alarm bells off but after the day's events I was not thinking straight.

I didn't know what to say to her statement because with it being so long since the death of Jane and having had Lindsey with me so much I had started to look at her romantically, but I had held those thoughts suppressed deep inside by telling myself it was just me desperately grabbing for a replacement for the love that I had lost. With that I did feel a need for something or one to hold more than at that moment I could handle and very quickly we were wrapped in a passionate embrace and kissing with such passion. One thing led to another and before long we were laying naked in each other's arms touching and caressing each other. Then as if by magic I felt a sudden bout of guilt and turned myself away from her. "We lay there me wrapped in guilt over what we had come so close to doing while at the same time wondering why I was feeling this way as there was absolutely nothing for me to feel guilty for. After all Jane was dead and buried whilst Lindsey was laid beside me naked wanting nothing more than to share and satisfy my sexual desires. We cuddled for a while before my coming to the conclusion that for us to become intimate would be completely wrong, so dressing again and leaving my bedroom with Lindsey still laid naked in my bed clearly disappointed at coming so close to what she wanted.

As I walked out from the bedroom and into the passageway that led into the lounge I noticed a note lying on the floor by the front door so I stooped over and picked it up. Being late afternoon I could plainly see it was not delivered by the post man so taking it with me I re-joined Lindsey who had got up and was sitting on my couch before opening the note up to read it. Reading it I suddenly felt a deep sense of betrayal by me on Jane and my hands started to tremble. Seeing my anguish Lindsey snatched the note from my hands to read it herself. Once read she crumpled it up throwing it into the waste paper bin beside the couch.

"What do we do now Mike?" she asked after reading the note, "You know I can't keep it secret any more and you know how I feel about you. I don't know what to do because Jane is and will always be my best friend, but why can't she stay dead so I can have you" Looking back at her I was confused as I myself had grown feelings for Lindsey but I had a much deeper love for Jane. "Well!" I said, "Its best we wait until the eclipse and see what may happen coz it seems to be important." But what was so important about the eclipse I asked myself. Once Lindsey had departed I dug through the rubbish in my bin and finding the note retrieved it. Taking it over to my couch I opened it out and read it again. I know you looked for me on the stores camera tape the letter said but remember you and Lindsey are the only ones who can see me for now. You'll need Johns help very soon because of someone we hadn't anticipated. The note was written and signed by Jane.

The eclipse was due on the 11th of August and it was still only the 15th of June so we had to wait for another eight weeks to find out what was going to happen. All I could do was hope that when the time came I would be able to do what was necessarily and not mess it up, more importantly could Lindsey be relied on not to try anything to stop Jane from returning in an attempt to have me for herself.

Over the next few weeks our time was spent looking everywhere for any sign of Jane but nothing until on the first of July when her spirit reappeared to me. It was during the night in a dream that I saw Jane standing in the road where she had died. The image in my head showed just her walk out of a cloud of mist into the light of day. One thing that did strike me as strange about it was the quick flashes of a calendar with the 11th of August circled and a time written under it. This was the exact time of the forecasted eclipse of the sun. That image stayed in my head even after awaking the following morning.

Once up taking Jane's note with me I went straight to the police station asking for D.C Ammet (John) who I knew would be on duty. An officer picked up a phone and called John who quickly arrived taking me into an interview room so as to enable us to talk uninterrupted. I handed him the note that had been slid under my door on the previous day which he read very scrupulously. After finishing the note, he looked over his tidy desk and said, "If this note warned you of someone unexpected how do you know that you can trust me? After all I'm a detective that you've only recently met." "Because the note said that I will need your help when the time comes" was my quick reply. "So got any ideas of who this note warns you of?" was his next question to which I had no idea. After several more questions we jotted down a list of four people's names that had any idea of what was going on. The names were the two of us Lindsey and of course Jane herself but there was a possible fifth who we simply called X. With my mind already puzzling over the X factor John out of the blue started asking about Lindsey and my relationship with her. After reading the note again more carefully John brought something to my attention that I hadn't even dreamt of before" Have you considered the possibility that the note may not even be warning you of an unknown person, but perhaps someone you do already know X and they will do something unanticipated? Say maybe Jane's ex-boyfriend. I know that he is serving time for his assault on her and it was you that stopped him, or maybe it refers to Lindsey and her feelings for you. From my past women can be very devious when it comes to matters of the heart; Either way I'll make some enquiries and let you know if I turn anything up." With that we said our goodbyes and I left the police station heading home still thinking of the notes warning and of course Lindsey.

Once back in the quiet of my home I made myself a drink sat down, and thought for a long time about Jane, myself and Lindsey and where we all were in everything that was happening. I had fallen asleep by the time that right on schedule I became aware of Lindsey coming through the front door. The first thing she did was to kiss me very passionately and tell me how much she had missed me that day and how much I would of enjoyed being on her days' photo-shoot because it was for lingerie for a mail order catalogue. It felt as though she was acting like a loving wife, partly my own fault because with everything that was going on I gave her Jane's door key so that she could let herself straight in. Trying hard to ignore my attraction to her I did my best to avoid any sign of flirting by her while talking about Jane or fixing my attention on the T.V set. It was about nine o'clock when the phone rang and it was John on the other end checking if I was home because he had some information for me. When I told him that Lindsey had made him a drink and sat down to listen to his news. He started by informing me that David (Jane's ex) had been released from his incarceration and was currently living with his new girlfriend. More than that was his girlfriend had asked associates about Jane and me why was unknown so he was definitely still in the running as our mysterious X. So to was Linsey because she had been heard telling a work colleague that she wanted and intended to make me hers within as short a time as possible although that was also unconfirmed. Hearing this did make me feel somewhat uneasy but I knew that while still alive the two women had been like sisters but there was the night that Lindsey had felt everything when Jane used her body so as to make love with me again. Maybe Lindsey thought that I was making love with her and my feelings had changed. Before he left I opened myself up and told John everything which he took in astounded and I think somewhat flabbergasted and actually spoken with her but again nothing has been confirmed." Not knowing just what the time was you could of knocked John down with a feather when out of the mirror that hung on the wall came a cloud of mist like water seeping out of a spring and out stepped Jane.

After composing himself John stammered in the best friendly police man voice he could," So you must be the elusive Miss Thompson that has been causing such a mystery around here." Before either of us could speak again Jane replied with, "Yes I am Jane and I am very pleased meet you John, you're a good man." "How do you know my name? I've not told you." he responded to her answer. "Here we know everybody's name, now listen to what I can tell you because I don't have much time left." came Jane's next statement which had both John and I rooted to the spot where we were. Having our full attention, she continued with what she had to tell us. "It's almost time for my return but I need both your help Lindsey's life depends on what you do because she is about to receive some very bad news."

That night I could not sleep with worrying about Lindsey and very soon my eyes were crying until she arrived. "Oh my God sweetheart what is the matter?" I asked half expecting the news that Jane's spirit had warned me about the previous day. I was deeply saddened when she revealed that she had just returned from the local hospital where she had an appointment with a consultant who had informed her that she had cancer, bad news in itself but much worse because it was grade four breast cancer meaning that she had little time left to live maybe only months. "Will Jane be on the other side and will we still be best friends like before? She asked in a frightened tone trying not to cry before adding something that made me question myself. We talked until quite late about what was left of her life, how her parents and little brother would react knowing what would happen to her. Her last comment before falling asleep was going to stay with me for the rest of my life. She said "Why can't I take Jane's place with you and let her stay dead until I die." At that moment I would of very happily of done just that if she could be better again, but how could I turn away from Jane and everything that she meant to me.

After another sleepless night milling over all the things that the previous night had revealed to me I knew that I needed to see or at least talk with Jane. As so many in the past at 11.55 pm Jane's spirit appeared to me from out of the wall mirror in my lounge and let me know everything that had already happened that day. She could easily understand Lindsey's situation and wishes which was to lead on to what was to happen later. "Is there anything that I can do to save her? I asked desperately not wanting to lose her from my life as well. "No, nobody can do anything to help her yet, but be comforted because in a very short while she will be well and we can all be together again just as we were before I died. I know this my love so don't fret." We were able to talk a little more before she faded back into the mirror again leaving me more at ease but not able to say a word to Lindsey.

I made the decision to let Lindsey know nothing of it while playing along with her wishes so as to give her some happiness during her last days. That would be difficult to do while staying faithful to my Jane but at least I only had ten more days to go until the eclipse. As it turned out that was relatively easy that is until the Sunday before the eleventh when after a late night at the local club with her I woke up to find out that I had not returned hone but was at Lindsey's place and in her bed with her. I remember asking myself what I had done. Had I spent the night having sex with her, I wish that I could remember what happened and why I was in the wrong bed lying next to the wrong woman. I managed to slide out of bed and dress before I sneaked from her room and left going home feeling very guilty over what I may have done the night before.

With only four more days to go before the eclipse and Jane's return from the grave I had the feeling of guilt over my night with Lindsey plus there was so much yet to do in preparation. I had not seen anything of John in over a week so I felt that I should contact him and check on preparations. After leaving a message on his answering machine I was just about to get myself a shower when I heard the sound of her coming in. Lindsey's made me nervous about what she might say or do. I opened the bathroom door only to be greeted by, "What the bloody hell happened to you last night? I got you drunk to get you home and make love all night but what did you do. You throw your guts up and crashed out. It took me ages to get your clothes off and into bed. And when you left this morning? And why didn't you wake me to say goodbye?" Feeling my guilt over the night before lifted I quickly responded with, "I'm very sorry. I must have drunk more than I should of and I can't apologise enough for being so sick." The telephone ringing gave me a reason to go back into the lounge to answer it was from John who hearing her in the background just said, "Can you come to the station his afternoon because I need to ask you a few more questions concerning Miss Thompson."

That afternoon dressed in cut-off jeans and T-shirt I walked to the police station alone where John was waiting for me. "Good you haven't got you know who with you. We have some important things to discuss and I don't want her knowing about them." he said in his official detective voice, I think as much for himself as me especially after his first contact with a ghost (Jane). Once in his office he could talk to me more freely which he very quickly did starting with, "About Thursday I've managed to get the stretch of road you are going to require closed for several hours but any longer will cause serious problems. That was one potential snag sorted out now there were more to make sure of Lindsey. "Now as for Lindsey we had to come up with an excuse to firstly keep her away from where I would be and secondly stop her from interfering in any way. That would be a problem so we decided to think it over for the next couple of days. Before leaving him John told me how he had written a letter to himself with a photograph holding a newspaper with the date showing as confirmation detailing everything and would give it to me on the Wednesday night. With only that night, Tuesday, Wednesday and Thursday to go I could really do with some help in finding a way to get rid of Lindsey for the eclipse.

That night as if in an answer to my prayers Jane appeared to me in my bedroom. As if she already knew what troubled me she said, "I think I should use Lindsey again so we can make love like before." "But she will feel it to. And you will experience me being unfaithful to you." I replied to which she came back with, "But for her after the eclipse it wont of happened so how will she be able to remember something that hadn't happened yet for her and besides it may be her body but it will be me that you're making love with." Thinking of it that way it was a good idea but that still left me knowing that I had made love to another and I still had the problem of how to get away on the Thursday. Baring that in mind I was able to face Lindsey on the Tuesday without worrying too much about what she may do.

As it was the Tuesday came and went with relatively no problem until the evening when a couple of things happened. First came a visit from John about seven o'clock handing me a letter addressed to himself asking me to personally hand it back to him after Thursday's eclipse, and secondly he told me not seemingly excited explaining that she had a visit from Jane's spirit the night before asking her if she could share her body again to have sex with me. Knowing that I had already arranged it in rough with Jane I pretended to be surprised but went along with it. "We will have to wait until Jane's spirit shows before we can make love" I said before Lindsey came back with, "Why wait for her? I can please and love you." "No" I said "If We are going to be together and let Jane stay dead I think it best she has one last chance of being one with me."

It was plane for me to see that she wanted me for herself for the little remaining time that she still had, but I wasn't going to give up on Jane even though it could be so easy to do so by just not being at the place that she died and letting her soul go forever. No I wasn't going to give up that easily. We had shared so many trials and tribulations together to conveniently simply let her go for another bearing in mind the fact that if Jane had not died then Lindsey would not even be attracted to me, plus I do not believe that could I cope with losing Lindsey to cancer if nothing was done.

I made an excuse and left Lindsey in the lounge watching the T.V while I went to my bedroom where I called John and asked what he had planned to pick her up" Now I knew what I had to do but how could I keep her busy until morning. "Why are you coming for her?" I asked to which he used the excuse of taking her to a specialist who might be able to treat her very serious condition. As far as she would know he had been using the telephone and calling in favours from people he knew to get her the help that she would be needing over the time that she had left. This news gave me an idea so on returning to her I crossed my fingers behind my back and made a commitment to her that would diminish the risk of her spoiling things the next day. "Lindsey. I've been doing a lot of thinking and have decided that I want to marry you and forget about Jane." With that news her face lit up like a Christmas tree and swung her arms around me saying that she wanted to tell her family and friends straight away and move in with me as soon as possible. I just hoped even prayed that Jane knew and agreed with my actions knowing that in 24 hours all this would never have happened. I took her to the bedroom and laid her down on hearing coffee being stirred by Jane to let me know that she was in the kitchen and wanted to see me so I sat myself down on the couch only to find my ass landing in a car seat right next to Jane. This time unlike so many times in the past we were not driving head long into the inevitable crash but was Stationary. "What's happening?" I asked in total surprise. "Do you trust me asked Jane? to which I answered ""With my life." "When its time avoid being near Lindsey because she thinks you want to be with her and I will not come back." "I know. Its tearing me apart letting her believe it, she never would if I were still here and her best mate." "No, and if everyone does what is needed I will still be here alive and with you all again." reassured Jane making me feel confidant of my future. In the blink of an eye I was again sitting on my couch. At this particular time, I wanted so badly to tell Lindsey that she was not going to die of cancer as a sort of reward for her help in allowing her deceased best friend live and love again but if I did there was no guarantee that she wouldn't do everything to prevent things happening as planned.

For now, I had to avoid anyone and anything that could prevent my being free for the eclipse. On the morning of the right day I rushed to the window to see how bright it was outside but we had total cloud cover which had me worried that the eclipse not being visible might obstruct my being at the right place and at the right time. I need not of been concerned as the eclipse would still happen and my Jane would before long be with me again. Getting dressed quickly I made myself a cup of tea and picked up the telephone and called John to confirm that he was indeed keeping Lindsey busy and the stretch of road needed clear to which he told me yes and wished he luck on the day. With a quiet confidence and spring in my step I walked out of my or more like our home and leisurely strolled down along the road outside which joined onto the main road into the town where the crowds of people were looking for their best spot to witness the upcoming eclipse. Stopping every few metres and looking upward at the clouds and asking myself, was this for real or was I about to wake up and find out that nothing had changed and I was only dreaming. I didn't even notice a group of three of my neighbours trying to attract my attention to invite me to join them in their eclipse watch. And then it happened, just as I reached the spot where a year before I had lost my everything I was back in the car sitting next to Jane driving along the road toward the inevitable crash, but this time I told Jane to push down the brake pedal just in time to avoid hitting the tractor trailer that was in the process of reversing back out of a fields gateway. This time she was not only wearing the same designer dress that she was modelling but just as the year before it was raining and I knew that this was what I had been dreaming of. She looked over at me and said in a grateful way, "I knew you would save me and bring me back my darling, now everything should be back a year and we have an eclipse to look forward to."

CHAPTER 5

My beautiful Jane was alive again and back at my side where she wanted to be but I was still aware of everything that had happened during the previous twelve months that now had not happened yet. More than that I knew that she was pregnant with my child or was she? And what about Lindsey and John they both knew what was going to happen but would they remember because for them it had not happened. "Let's go home now my love and celebrate my rebirth." Said Jane to which I agreed. "Seeing as we have twelve months to relive maybe we should spend them in bed having sex" I came out with to which Jane's reply was, "mmmmmmm that sounds good to me." showing the same warmth and love that I knew and loved along with a very sexy twinkle in her eyes. Yes, my love was back.

One thing that I had completely forgotten about was the x factor person, who was it and why were they a threat to Jane's returning. On pulling up outside of our flat the look of relieve at coming home on her face was a picture that I will always treasure. We entered our flat and straight away flung our arms around each other and kissed like never before as we started to undress each other to make love.

After a long night of passion and a late breakfast I surprised Jane when from out of my jacket I pulled out the sealed letter that John had given me to hand to him after the eclipse. Opening the envelope, she pulled out firstly a photograph of her opened grave and a hand written letter describing everything plus another photograph of him holding a copy of a national newspaper showing the day's date now in a years' time." You cannot give this to him or our lives will become the topic news stories everywhere, and we don't want that." She was obviously right so finding something to light it with I burned it all. Now we could get on with our lives just like everyone else and what happened would become nothing more than a story, but first I wanted to visit the graveyard and see the spot where her grave had been.

As we walked up the pathway toward the church and its well looked after graveyard Jane wanted to know how much of the coming year I remembered because she was hoping that we could book our wedding for a time that we knew the sun would be shining for us. As we reached the right spot we saw that there was an empty space where Jane had been buried, the sight of which brought tears to my eyes as I remembered the pain and upset that I had endured. So far everything was turning out perfect but there was still one person who I needed to see and check on, Lindsey so Jane borrowed my mobile phone and called her to invite her out for a drink that night. During that evening mainly the girls talked about whatever girls talk about, fashion, music, movies and of course boys but my heart almost missed a beat when Lindsey started telling Jane a dream she had where she had died and come back to life during the eclipse that had just occurred. "It was so real that I seriously believed it actually happened but it couldn't of or did it."

It appeared that for the second time it was the 12th August 1998 only this time Jane was alive and with me with our whole lives ahead of us after the magical occurrence during the full eclipse the day before and now due to happen again only 12 months later. After 1 spending a whole year feeling the pain of having the one I love more than anything killed in a tragic car accident and then returned to me, all I wanted was to thank God by allowing me to do something good with time being rewound a year to live again. With that, I was happy at knowing my love would be discovering that she was pregnant with the child that would have never be born if not for the magic of the full eclipse and God's grace.

When I looked at Jane my thoughts straight away turned my attention over to how we could make the coming repeat of the previous year be a happier one than the one where she had been dead. Her just being alive again for me was more than I could possibly dream of yet she was and we had the gift of reliving a whole year. Before her accident during the day I would have gone to go to work filling the shelves in a local supermarket and Jane was due to meet her modelling agent about working with her best friend Lindsey, modelling for a travel agent before the following holiday season.

We kissed goodbye at the door before heading off in opposite directions, me for my motorbike and Jane to her car to go to our days' work. I rode to the end of our road and turned left heading onto the one way shopping street past the turning toward the church where we had decided that we wanted to get married and the graveyard where she had laid to rest after her death, past the public house where Jane Lindsey and I would often unwind after a busy day's work with a drink and snack and finally past the turning into the police station where I had spent 24 hours and met John the police detective who had ,questioned me the year before but about to be relived after Jane's body had apparently been exhumed and for which I had been held as a suspect.

For obvious reasons I tried not to show the joy in my heart on this particular day but all day long colleagues were asking why I was so happy with comments like "have you won the lottery and are you on happy pills." It felt quite unreal to me how on this day the year before I had been in hospital, feeling the trauma of an accident and losing the girl I loved killed at my side, yet now it had never happened, even so I could not resist calling Jane just to tell her how much I loved her at lunchtime.

With the working day over I quickly returned home where Jane, having beaten me back, had cooked us a meal. After eating a simple meal of pie and mash potato she phoned her best friend to talk more about the day's meeting with their modelling agent, while I cleared the table before snuggling up on our couch to watch a movie and then turning in for the night. This was basically the way our lives were going, until on the 21st of that month, when at 7.30 in the morning we received an unexpected telephone call from John, the police detective who had arrested me over Jane's grave being dug up asking to visit us later that morning.

With a mixture of intrigue and nervousness by the phone call from John, one which was a total surprise to us both, Jane and I waited in our lounge awaiting him with trepidation and nervousness at what might be about to happen. "How does he remember what happened before my death and then return to life?" asked Jane, clearly frightened at the possible consequences if made public knowledge. At 11.45 in the morning John knocked at our door heralding his arrival, so with Jane standing sheepishly behind me, I opened it not knowing what to expect.

After giving the customary hello and welcome he held up a package and asked if he could come in and talk with us. Before allowing him to enter I looked over his shoulder to see if he was alone and we were not about to be inundated by the police. Apart from his parked unmarked private Honda civic car, there was not a sign of anyone so I beckoned him in, leading him into our lounge. He was wearing a pair of black casual trousers, a plain red sweat shirt and ordinary shoes which were not what one would expect from a police officer.

Leading the way I made a point of noticing how John was looking all around while seeming not to know where he was going, not having any knowledge of where he was now. "Do you not recognise us or our home John?" asked Jane clearly uncertain as to why he was there in the first place. "Not as far as I know, do you know me?" but in light of the contents of the wrapped package he was carrying, for me to open that might change. I accepted it with hesitation and carefully peeled back the edge of the wrapping paper to discover a shoebox sized box.

"Before you open it, please understand that I am not here in any official capacity but more like in the manner of a curious friend searching for answers." He said like a schoolboy wanting an answer from his teacher to a difficult problem. Before opening up the wrapped up box I looked at the writing on the wrapping and asked "Who wrote this to you?" almost afraid to ask or know. "It is my own hand writing that you see there but I never sent it to my knowledge or did I? I hope that you two can spread some light on it.

"How can we help you? Neither of us knows what or why you would send yourself something" said Jane, trying to appear as naively innocent as she could. "Open it and see what there is." came his calm response, so being somewhat curious myself, I gently lifted off the box lid and peered inside.

Inside it I found a mass of papers, photographs what resembled official reports with a cassette tape and a hand written letter in John's own writing addressed to himself."Why on earth would anyone send themselves a letter or package?" I asked trying to appear as ignorant on the subject as I could.

On John's urging, Jane went into our kitchen to make us all a pot of tea, while I picked out the small number of photos and sat back on our couch to browse over them. The first picture was a close up of a grave stone with written on it the words `here lays the body of Jane Thompson tragically taken from us on the 11th August 1998 but never forgotten` which had been taken only a few days previously for us. Next was a photograph taken from a short distance away showing an open grave, complete with an open coffin and cordoned off by police crime scene tape with John standing beside it holding up a newspaper, showing the date only a matter of days previously. Jane was sitting beside me trying to look surprised and shocked but not that well asked what this was all about. "What has it got to do with me?" Jane asked, while swiping at her long, wavy blonde hair from her eyes. "I think a lot more than you want to tell." John replied. Unexpectedly he handed me an official coroner's report congratulating us on our coming baby, a baby which was not going to be found out about for a few more weeks yet. Not thinking I slipped up and immediately thanked him, not remembering that she had only just conceived but it had not yet been confirmed.

Sounding pleased with himself John said, "So it's all true and has happened just as all this information says, you did die and have come back to life. There must be a reason why, perhaps you have a destiny to fulfil." Pausing to look at our faces he carried on with, "So that explains why when I went to the church earlier and looked around the graveyard there was not a sign of any open grave or tomb stone with Jane's name on it. All this stuff confirms that time has in some way been altered, to bring you back." said John in a mixture of both relief and bewilderment.

Although I think we were all asking ourselves the same question it was Jane in her inquisitive way who said "I don't understand why or how you have all this stuff now because now nothing has happened. I have not died and come back to life. So tell me why you think you know this John and what are you going to do about it?"

Taking a deep breath, he made us unsure about the future when he said "It appears that I am meant to know everything what has happened with you otherwise the contents of this box would not still be here." Pausing and looking directly into our faces he went on to say," I suspect there is another reason why I have been allowed to know all this, perhaps your experience with death and return to life connects you Jane to something else equally as miraculous." His statement filled our minds with much as we tried to think of why we had been contacted and how John had known what had happened plus did anybody else know.

After about another hour of talking, it was decided that concerning Jane and I, it was best that nobody else could ever know about it, so in our presence, John burnt the evidence of everything that had happened which he had brought in the box with him, Also we decided to keep in touch in case anything new happened. By new I mean ghostly or supernatural and by the December nothing had occurred worthy of our paying attention to so the two of us set about preparing for the festive break not knowing that things were about to happen, things that affect all of our lives including that of Lindsey's.

It was as the chimes from the town's sixteenth century clock tower started to ring in the coming New Year, just like it had done the year before when Jane's ghost had first appeared to me while beside her grave. Only this time it was as Lindsey was raising her glass to toast the future as we entered the year of 1999 again when Jane seemed to suddenly freeze where she was sitting, with her face turning bluer and a completely blank look appeared on her face before her mouth opened to speak; only the voice we heard was that of an older lady with great sadness in it. Lindsey being frightened stopped in mid-sentence and her mouth dropped as we heard the woman's voice say, "God used the power of the eclipse to bring Jane back from the dead so please do it again and save the children, and the others," finishing off with "I'm begging you to please help them." Then Jane collapsed into my arms and thankfully for us nobody else where we were had noticed anything. It was only a matter of seconds before she came around again saying, "What happened?" when her eyes opened "are we being called on babe?"

Turning to face me she told me what had just happened to her asking what could we do, to which I suggested telling John and seeing if he could help us to identify the woman whose spirit had just appeared to her. I was not too sure about calling him because of the nature of why, but I think we both knew that if we were being called on to prevent the deaths of many, we would almost certainly be needing his help. For the rest of the night, we managed to dismiss what had just happened as foolish tomfoolery as a result of our drinking, but our talk was filled of questions mostly from Lindsey about what she had seen happen to her best friend and coming back to life with the eclipse because for everyone else including her it was about six months in the future that it was due.

For Jane and myself we were more concerned about discovering who's involved, the where it was happening where ever it was and more importantly when and why. It must of been about five in the morning that we arrived back home, after swearing Lindsey to secrecy, whilst warning her of the potential dangers to all of us if the wrong people found out any of it. When we reached home I left a message for John on his answering machine asking him to contact us then Jane and I went to bed our minds full of thoughts of what had happened to her earlier.

Come morning we were not surprised when John knocked on our door carrying a note book ready for making notes if needed when we shared with him the news following the previous night. "Mrs Sarah Donaldson is or was her name, the woman we need to trace who contacted me." relayed Jane as she told of our experience and the plea for help from beyond, that she had received as we and Lindsey drank the New Year in.

"Well I guess I can run a trace on her name and see what I can find out about her, do you have any idea as to when she died or how?" said John, intrigued by what he had just heard. "All I can say is she's called Sarah Donaldson and I could smell burning fuel and bodies" added Jane. As we spoke I was amazed at how John being a big built man and able to portray such authority and control just sat there on our couch mesmerized by what he was learning. Until we knew about Sarah Donaldson, where she died, how she died and who the children that her spirit wanted us to save were. There was little that we could do other than wait for news from John on his investigation to identify her. Also we couldn't forget the fact that I had a job to go to and for the girls they had their modelling work to keep them busy and for Jane herself she had to put her unborn baby first.

Keeping the task that we had embarked on fresh in my mind at all times I had to carry on as normal with my usual daily routine so I kissed Jane goodbye and set off to my job at a local supermarket. As I walked up the main street past the shoe shop, the opticians, WH Smiths, Peacocks clothes store and a branch of Lloyds bank, I couldn't help but ask myself if what we were doing was intended by God because if successful many souls would not be going to the other side as had already happened during the past year.

"Mike! Wait for me." came Lindsey's voice calling from the window of a bus as it slowed to stop at its stop outside of a newsagent's shop. "Are you at home tonight because I have been offered a job posing for some posters advertising an air show at the county show this year."

At that time nobody could have known that the very same air show that Lindsey would be promoting through her modelling work would be the same venue that Jane was asked to save the children at by the spirit of Sarah Donaldson. We carried on walking along together until I had to turn off for my work and she crossed the road and round a bend leading to a crescent where all along the outer edge were offices of the town council and legal firms, while on the inner side was a grassed area with seating for walkers. This was the same area where Jane and I often had sat and talked a lot after her near rape experience before leaving school and finding love with me.

Arriving at my work I was just about to enter when my mobile phone let me know that I had just received a text message, which on checking, was from Jane, informing me that John was going to stop by on his way home after coming off duty that night to let us know what he had found out from his checking on Sarah Donaldson. She also informed me she had started to suffer from morning sickness over half way through her pregnancy. Hearing from him I hoped would let us know who she was and with luck where to look for the coming saving from death of many. With that I found the rest of the day seeming to pass quite quickly and soon I was leaving work and going home again, to prepare for our coming visitors that night.

Walking through the front door I was greeted by Jane throwing her arms around me before leading me into the lounge where John and Lindsey were waiting. "Hi guys what's the news." I asked, "I've been tracing as many Sarah Donaldson's as I can." Was the reply from John to my question "I have found three people so far, one is a ninety-three-year-old from Scotland, one is an eighteen-year-old student from London and the other is a fifty-four-year-old junior school teacher from a place called Haleigh in the county of Suffolk. From what you have told me so far I suspect that she must be the Sarah Donaldson who we are looking for but for what?" said John in his detective voice. With that, we all sat down around our lounge discussing what we should be doing now until late into the night when something happened to clarify our goal.

During the course of our conversation, John informed us that he soon expected to be busy policing a future protest action by those protesters set against a company that were planning to do some exploratory fracking drilling on the waste ground just outside of the town. "What's fracking?" I asked trying not to appear too stupid in front of the others. "I'm not too sure, but I believe it's about getting gas out of the rock in the ground below us." He replied. "I've heard about that" said Lindsey, continuing with "I saw a news report blaming it for causing small earthquakes somewhere that does not normally get them." "Whether it does or not we can bet that whoever does it will pay an expert to say it's safe. It'll be the likes of the police to stop the protesters." We all hoped that the company wanting to drill would change its mind and decide not to do anything.

At that time Lindsey talked Jane into going with her when she posed for the air show advertising, in a selection of different pilot uniforms from various countries, past and present. After getting back home again she described the different outfits saying that she should get one because it looked quite sexy followed by one of her winks and naughty smile. I remember thinking that if she did I certainly would not mind.

It was at 11.55pm when all of us started to smell burning fuel and flesh. Raising her hand over her nose Jane managed to say "What on earth is going on here, it smells like burning skin and petrol." And then it happened, something that would devastate and haunt us for the rest of our lives. It was, as I said, 11.55pm when we started to smell burning fuel and flesh and we were wanting to know its source that our attention was drawn to an image of I guess Sarah Donaldson. She said only a few words which were "Remember what you will see and make the right choice." Then a very bright flash of light briefly dazzled all of us and on being able to see again we discovered that we had somehow been placed amongst the massive crowd of spectators watching a display of Ariel manoeuvring by two world war one bi planes entertaining them.

As we watched one of the planes clip the others tail end, causing it to break off sending the plane plummeting toward earth. More than that was the plane was right over a long wooden stand with seating for the onlookers. Amid the screams of horror everyone started clambering to get clear, tripping over each other and pushing in panic to escape from what was about to happen.

As the plane fell I, could see the brave pilot wrestling with the controls trying to steer it clear, with little success. None of the four of us could move, meaning that we were about to be at the centre of the crash. Jane and Lindsey screamed in horror while John and I struggled with our legs trying to move and expecting to die. The pilot was managing to direct the plane clear but it was no use because the plane smashed straight into a parked fuel tanker behind the stand.

The whole sky lit up as the tanker exploded into a huge ball of flame which engulfed the whole length of the stand where the four of us were caught like the over a hundred and fifty other people unable to get clear and were being turned into figures of flame. Although we were unable to move from where we stood, the wave of fire that flowed across the entire stand never touched us enabling us all see what the crowd saw as they were dying. It was John who first noticed that at one end of the stand were a party of junior school aged children with staff on a day excursion from their school.

After we had witnessed the catastrophe, another bright light returned us our lounge where the girls clung onto each other, traumatised by what we had seen, while both John and I fell to the floor, speechless by what we had just seen. "How can something so bad be allowed to happen to so many young children?" I managed to say while still crying at what we had seen.

"Maybe that is why you were contacted Jane, to put right what should never happen by God." said John, who was trying to make some sort of sense out of the whole thing. It didn't take much for us to know what we had to do and the reason why. I doubt that any of us were able to get any sleep that night and we could not dare tell anyone, which meant that we could never get professional help with dealing with it.

CHAPTER 6

By the morning I believe that we all knew what we had to do, but to be honest, I had no idea how we could stop one plane from causing another one to crash unintentionally. Basically we had to prevent the accident to save 138 lives, including 56 children, by stopping the crash from happening. As I made a pot of tea for Jane and I my mind was filled with what we had to do, until everything became unimportant, when Jane came out of our bedroom and told me of her night.

"Someone spoke to me in my sleep last night and now I'm not sure if we should do anything." "Not do anything! With all that we saw last night, what were you told?" I asked in disbelief at what she had just said, knowing that she was the sort of person who would gladly give her life for another who deserved to live. "It was a deep voice and it felt very cold and bad." Pausing she carried on with, "I think it was the devil and it wants their souls, what do we do, Mike?" After suggesting that we talk with John and Lindsey before we did anything I left her for work as I always did after breakfast.

During the day, John who had been finding out as much as he could about places that can put on air shows, like the one where the crash was due to happen so was somewhat surprised when we told him about Jane's dream message. When I told him he quite angrily said, "I don't understand, just think of the tens of thousands of people that die every year that we don't know in advance about but this time we do know everything that will happen before it does and we can stop it from ever happening. To me this one thing gives my life a sense of purpose. You can choose to do nothing because of a message in a dream, but I am going to do anything to save them kids."

Obviously he was quite right in what he said making me feel a little petty. He was right of course but all the same we were concerned as to what would happen if we helped. It was Jane who decided that we had to help, after she had been returned to life after she was killed a year before the full eclipse which is due to happen again this year. "Thank you John you just helped us understand what is at stake if we do nothing, so tell us what you have found out so far."

"The show is due to be held on the site of a world war one airfield in Kent and tomorrow I should know the names of the pilots involved. What we need to know is which pilot is the one who crashed and which one caused it because maybe we can stop him from flying." Before leaving our place John enquired about where Lindsey was that day and what would she be doing to help us. "She flew out of Heathrow this morning for a modelling assignment in the Caribbean and should be gone about a week."

"Lucky cow getting paid to work in the Sun and leave us with the cold and wet. I bet she comes back with a good tan on her" proclaimed John as he was leaving. Now we had committed ourselves to the task ahead, we called it a night and were preparing ourselves to go to bed and feeling like we were doing the right thing, not knowing that again Jane would get another message, this time while I was there, by means of an image in our wall mirror.

The image in the mirror resembled a silhouetted figure of a human saying "If you stop it happening, I will take your souls for mine. Just so you know that I will your friend will die very soon." Just as it finished speaking its eyes lit up, in a bright piercing red glow, which told us that an evil spirit had plans to steal many souls. Straight away Jane got on her mobile phone and rang Lindsey

After what felt like hours, from the other end of the phone came the very upset voice of Lindsey saying, "I should have stayed at home sis. There are so many dead and I was meant to be on the same bus that has crashed."

There had been a very traumatic crash killing everyone who was travelling on a bus where Lindsey was. As Jane consoled Lindsey I went over and switched on the TV putting on a 24hour news channel to see if there was any news, there was. It soon transpired that a bus which had been hired to transport guests to the Caribbean Paradise Hotel where Lindsey was booked in to stay during her work had ran off the road and over a cliff into a steep sided ravine killing all of the 43 passengers on board and the driver.

After ending her call Jane turned her head toward me and said, wiping the tears from her eyes, "All those people have been killed because we are trying to stop the plane accident. It's our fault it has happened and we almost lost my best friend as well. Maybe we shouldn't carry on with this." "We have to finish this; it's why you were contacted in the first place." "What if anyone else dies because of what we are doing? I wish I knew why out of all the deaths during the time after my return these people need to be saved?" Thinking for a moment for the right thing to say I ended with, "Try to think of it as a coincidence it happening then and the evil one took credit for it to scare us into doing what he wants us to do, and there must be a reason for saving them." We never told Lindsey or John what happened that night before the bus crash or I feel that they might think twice about helping us.

It was the second week of February and we were each making our own arrangements to spend our night at a Valentine's party or dance. Jane and I had tickets to go to my works staff do, John unfortunately was working and Lindsey was due to join in a party from her employers, but all was about to become a living hell for us.

We were just leaving home when the light in our lounge switched on suddenly without the switch being touched "What the heck has happened." said Jane dumbfounded by what had just happened, so I turned around and walked back into our lounge to check. The first thing that I noticed on entering our lounge was our TV which had turned on and then I saw our mirror, with a not right reflection in it.

"Jane! I called out, I think we are about to get a visitation from beyond. I could hear the sound of her coming back into our place as I watched a shear black shadow form in the centre of the screen with a pair of piercing red eyes appear. It didn't take much time for us to know where the reflection had come from, an evil one. Trying to look as calm and relaxed as she could Jane asked, "What do you want now, you evil piece of shit." I can tell that Jane was putting on an act because I was as frightened as she was.

"You ignored my warning before, now you can watch as I take your friends soul. With that the image in our mirror faded and another one formed. This one was one of the bedrooms where Lindsey was staying and we could see her sitting at her vanity table brushing her shoulder length straight hair before going to work. We could plainly see that whatever function she was planning to attend must be a big one by the expensive looking dress that she was laid out on her bed ready to put on.

Right there in our wall mirror we could see as Lindsey suddenly dropped her hair brush and lifted her hands against her cheeks seeming to scream. Although we couldn't see her face we could see its reflection in her vanity mirror and it looked so horrific when we saw her face literally melting away from her skull with her blood squirting in all ways as her eyeballs fall onto the floor before her body burst into flames where she stood. What we saw was so bad that Jane fainted into a heap on the floor and I rushed into our bathroom to be sick.

We had both seen that Hollywood special effects could mimic what we had seen that night but to actually see it happen for real was bad enough to drive some mad or even suicidal. For me personally I was reminded of how while Jane's spirit was in limbo between life and death it had used Lindsey's body to make love with me and how I had grown an extent of romantic love for her in the process. Now we had both just witnessed the deadly power of the evil one as she was dying in the most horrific way so far away from her home.

Jane had spent the night in tears over the murder of our friend and I had just sat staring at a bare wall trying to make sense out of what had happened. "Do you think that we should call John and tell him what happened last night because I am sure that he will find out at some point today?" I asked before picking up the phone to call him. I needn't have asked because before I could call our phone rang and it was him. "Have you seen the news today?" "I guess it's about Lindsey's murder last night."

"How do you know that?" he asked "I'll explain later." was my reply to him. After saying he was on his way over I called Jane informing her of our coming guest.

"How is she?" was the first thing that John asked when he arrived and then she walked out of our bedroom her face all puffy after crying so much at her loss. "We saw it all taking place John. She was killed by that bastard evil one as punishment for us not giving up on saving all those people."

There was a silence for a while before John continued with, "On the TV news the Authorities say that they think she was scarified as part of some sort of Satanist ritual but they have nothing to go on so far to find the guilty. Her remains will be flown back home during the next few days. I'll let you know where and when her funeral is when I can so you can go to show your respect." That evening the two of us spoke a lot about whether or not to continue with our task of saving those killed by the biplane crash or leave it to prevent any more deaths by the evil one. By the morning we had decided that to quit was not what Lindsey would have done so carrying on would be a way of honouring her memory.

A week later on the fifth day of March we received a call from John informing us of the funeral of our friend so we made the necessary arrangements to be there to pay homage to her memory. We stood their heads bowed in a certain amount of guilt because she had only died because of our determination to prevent the deaths of so many innocents who had already died in the pre eclipse time. "I wish I knew that we are doing the right thing." commented Jane wiping another tear from her eye while thinking of her best friend. "You are" came a comforting voice in both of our heads continuing with "You must save them because the child of the grand child of one of them is destined to save all life on earth from destruction by those that allow their greed for profit and power overrule everything that I intended for humanity. Do this and your friend will be returned."

If we succeed in preventing the deaths Lindsey will be brought to life again. Both of us were very happy and relieved at what we had been told, but we could not see anyone except the mourners, even so we knew who was talking to us. Now we knew the importance of what we were doing and we felt justified in our actions. Looking around at the other mourners I saw apart from her family and relatives, several of our school class mates, her agent from her work, a local photographer who she had modelled for and a newspaper journalist covering the funeral for a national paper.

When we got home I cut out from a newspaper a tribute to Lindsey that had been printed along with a photograph of her as a reminder of how much she meant to all of us before placing it in a frame which I found unused in a box of bits and pieces in the bottom of a kitchen cupboard, before fixing it to the lounge wall to the side of our TV.

The next day I told John about our experience at the funeral which made him as happy as we were, more so because we had decided to carry on and finish what we had started but because of what happened to Lindsey he more or less insisted that from then on Jane should not be involved in any way. Obviously she was not happy about his suggestion until he pointed out the fact that she was going to be a mother soon and our baby was too important.

"You do not want the same thing as happened to Lindsey to happen to your baby or you." he said, which had me contented by his concern for Jane and our unborn baby. I suggested that Jane visited her mother for a little time while John and I checked out a new night club on the edge of town that was beginning to get visited by many under aged children and was attracting unsavoury older men. This was a concern to the police but being monitored by them already along with the club owners. Under this excuse the two of us were able to make plans for how on earth to stop a plane from crashing and killing so many without Jane becoming involved or even knowing what we were doing.

Sitting in a local Mc Donald's take away with a cup of tea John took out his note book and started flicking through the pages until he found the page that he wanted. " I've found out as much as I can about the pilots involved. One and I believe the one who died was a retired RAF pilot is called James Morris with over 30 years of service to the crown. The other one is a rich want to be amateur that has used with his own money to learn to fly himself. He can fly but does not have the necessary skill to perform the split second manoeuvres being planned." "So what we need to do is find a way to stop their display from being used and prevent what we all saw from happening." I replied to his information. Bearing that in mind, we knew what was going to happen, we had to come up with an idea of how to stop the collision with the inevitable outcome.

Getting home again my mind was filled with ways to stop the crash without going against the law or harming either pilot to stop them flying. I wanted so much to talk with Jane and hear her thoughts on what to do but we had to keep her from knowing our plans and preventing them from being found out by the evil one.

After having something to eat the two of us settled down on our couch so that Jane could tell me about her day. "Hey guess what, I've been asked to model some maternity clothes by a store." "That's great sweetheart, you can get paid for having a bump." I replied jokingly." Oh I've got an appointment at the hospital for a scan tomorrow afternoon and we need to decide if we want to know the sex of our baby in advance of the birth. I'd rather not know in advance." I agreed with her as long as it was ok. We talked some more before at 11.55pm the smell of burning fuel and flesh filled our nostrils and an image of Sarah Donaldson followed by one of a fuel tanker. Come morning I somehow knew that Jane had received a message or instruction in her sleep which was shown when she said. "Think of preventing the explosion instead of the crash it may be easier. You might have to let a pilot die to save the others."

Three days later on the Friday night John came around to discuss what I had decided on doing as we were getting closer to the air show date. "Jane has been told in a dream that we should forget the planes and concentrate on the tanker, and another thing is our baby's due date is the twenty ninth of May only a couple of days before the air show."

The next day I accompanied Jane to the hospital situated in the next town for her scan to check on the development of our coming baby. I will never forget the feeling of pride with my darling Jane and I too on hearing the heartbeat. When the consultant carrying out the scan said that it looked healthy and with nothing to be concerned over we were both over the moon. "Why don't we go and visit your parents and let them that their grand-child is going to be ok." I said trying to curtain the joyful feelings inside under control while at the same time being a certain amount scared at the threat of death made by the evil one against my beautiful loving fiancée before killing our dear friend Lindsey.

Whilst we appeared to be living a usual life with me going to my work and Jane doing her modelling maternity clothes for a national clothing chain and whilst having her belly get larger with our child growing inside of her, John was busy gathering all the necessary information that would help us when it came time to act, like obtaining access to the cab of the tanker and where to find a spare key to start the engine in order to move it. As he said it felt as if we were planning some sort of criminal enterprise and jokingly suggested arresting himself which did make us laugh knowing that doing so would save lives and would secure all of our futures.

On the day a few days before the end of May, John who having borrowed a police car under the pretence of escorting the school children's coach to the show through the heavy traffic, which was expected by the organisers. After collecting me on route we met the coach and drove to the show arriving in enough time for the show which was just starting with a display by the red arrows. At home, what we didn't know was that Jane was getting admitted to the maternity hospital as she had gone into labour a few days past her due date thanks to Lindsey who had agreed to be with her whilst I was not at home for her.

When the time finally arrived for action we knew that in a matter of minutes a plane was going to crash killing so many innocent people, but we had made our own plans to stop it from happening. John and I found our way to a suitable place to watch events unwind away from the spectators stand just in case we failed.

"I'm going to check out a few things." said John standing up and casually walking around behind the stand toward the fuel tanker. Wearing his officer's identification badge as a way of not being thought of as a criminal or as though he did not belong there, he tried the driver's side door and found it unlocked. In the air way up above us came the sound of the two bi-planes coming in to start their display so John carefully opened the tankers door and climbed up into the cab.

After checking it he found a spare ignition key tucked behind the sun blind and started the engine.

Suddenly there was a cracking sound from above accompanied by screams from the crowd as one plane caught the others tail, ripping it off and making it start to fall uncontrollably toward the earth along with the falling tail end of one of the planes. That was the signal John needed and he started the tankers engine driving it about fifty meters forward away from where we knew the plane would hit. As I plainly observed, rather than bailing out and falling safely with a parachute, the retired RAF pilot James Morris bravely stayed in the plane fighting with its controls trying to direct it away from the crowd. As the falling plane fell, it briefly disappeared from sight behind the crowds stand and then there was a loud thud as it hit. But this time there was no massive explosion and wave of fire killing everyone.

As the emergency crews rushed to the crash I saw a TV news reporter standing in front of the camera telling the viewers about what she had just witnessed, and the sudden surprise when out of the wreckage clambered the pilot without as much as a single scratch on him. After taking the time to bow to the onlookers James Morris strolled over to the reporter to give an interview starting with a question,

"Where is that man who just moved the tanker out of the way? He has just saved many lives through his act." But nobody could say who it was as no-one was meant to be in it or move it. "How did you avoid being hurt?" asked the reporter but his reply would have people asking questions for a long time to come.

He said, "I have no idea what happened to me up there but I swear that just before I hit the tanker, a massive hand appeared from out of nowhere and surrounded me until after I hit, keeping me safe, it was a miracle like the person who moved the tanker." "Does anyone know who it was because whoever it is was is not a worker from here? It's like they knew what was going to happen in advance." said the chief of the ground staff who had just arrived on the scene.

With that over, John and I made our way back to his car and departed the air field heading for home both of us feeling contented with our actions on that day. As he drove his car, John expressed how he wished he knew what, by saving the unknown child whose descendent would save the world, would have happened if we hadn't done anything. We had just joined the M5 motorway heading for Exeter when my mobile phone started ringing and on answering it I received even more good news. "Mike my darling, I am at the hospital, we've had a baby girl born at exactly seventeen minutes past one pm. I will be discharged in about two hours after all the necessary checks are done with her." "We should be close enough to pick her up if you want Mike." offered John which I excitedly accepted knowing that during the time taken to save any lives I had just become a father to a little girl. As we drove back John switched on the car radio to listen to some music catching an interview with the other pilot from the show claiming that he was not going to fly anymore because of what had and would almost certainly have happened because of his error at the show.

As we drove along the motorway we talked a lot about ourselves and our families, "I've been wondering about your sir name John, does it come from a different country because it sounds like it is?" I asked inquisitively. "It's from India, my family moved here about two hundred years ago.

Before collecting Jane from the maternity ward at the hospital, John wanted to stop off at his home so that he could change his clothes for his usual off duty ones which were jeans and sweat shirt. Whilst he did what he wanted to do I stayed in his police car and listened to the radio talking a lot about the incident at the air show and playing the recorded interview with the pilot who would now be dead, if not for the mysterious man that moved a fuel tanker in time to avoid a devastating explosion that could have killed dozens of people and the unexplainable feeling of being held as the plane crashed, protecting him from harm. When he returned I could sense a feeling of success in him as John got back into the car casually pulling out, heading for the hospital and Jane.

CHAPTER 7

After we had stopped to pick up a bouquet of flowers to give to Jane for when we collected her from the maternity hospital where she had been admitted earlier that day to give birth, we parked in the necessary space to collect her and then returned to our home, only to get another surprise. It was as we entered our front door with Jane walking a little unsteadily after giving birth, John carrying her case and I holding our baby, that Jane instantly noticed that the tribute to Lindsey which we had kept after her funeral had disappeared from where we had placed it on our lounge wall next to a framed photograph of the two of them taken on their last day of school.

"Have you taken down Lindsey's tribute darling?" asked Jane. I replied, "No babe, I haven't touched it." Then John being aware of past happenings suggested, "Maybe one of you should check out her grave or perhaps give her a call on her mobile." "That's a good idea; I'll try her number once we get mummy and baby sorted out. Oh, we had better decide on a name for her as well." I said. "After all that has happened to all of us this last year or so I think that we should call her Faith because we have had to have it, to do what has been required of us." Jane said in reply to me.

Looking down at our baby Faith she smiled seeming to approve of Jane's choice of name for her. With that decided on, I suggested the two of us take both sets of parents out for a meal to give them firstly Faith's name and secondly ask for their blessing to get married, but for now Jane wanted and needed to try and contact Lindsey.

We needn't have done anything about checking up on Lindsey as Jane's ringing mobile soon revealed. "I'm going to come and see you tomorrow because I need to pass on a message to you, Mike and if possible, John as well. I need to know what has happened to me, all I remember is sitting at the makeup mirror in my hotel room and then my face felt like it was on fire, then I was in a room surrounded by many others being led out one of two doors one by one. Was I dead again sis?" she said inquisitively before passing on her congratulations over her giving birth.

"I'll leave it to Mike to explain everything to you tomorrow Lin's, he knows what has happened and why. I'm just so happy that you have come back to us." said Jane obviously over joyed with knowing that her best friend had again escaped an early death. But first we had to feed and change Faith who was sleeping in her mothers` arms while she talked on the phone.

Another thing that John wanted to do was to telephone the junior school and enquire as to the reaction to the air show which came back with nothing but praise, and after seeing the pilot's interview on the t v thanks for the unknown person who had moved the tanker saving their lives.

Once arrangements had been made ahead of the following day May 29 1999 John said his goodbye's and left Jane and I for the rest of the day enabling us to do what all new parents do for our daughter. We also telephoned both sets of new grandparents to give them the good news of one more to add to our family trees and to arrange us all going out for an evening meal, trusting Lindsey and John's wife Carol to look after Faith for a few hours on the Saturday night.

At a little after two pm the following day Lindsey arrived and with tears of joy in her eyes Jane threw her arms around her friends neck hugging her as if she were a family member who had been away for many years. Once they had finished hugging Jane took her friend by the hand and led her into our lounge saying, "Come and meet Faith. Mike is holding her now so you can meet and hold our baby." Continuing with, "Will you be her God mother." I was just about to fill her in on everything when a knock at our door let us know that John had arrived so I temporarily, held talking to Linsey in order to answer it.

"Lindsey is alive and well again after what you did at the show my friend. She is here now." I said on opening the door, as if I had just spoken about his daughter or winning the lottery. On seeing him as we re-entered our lounge, Lindsey threw her arms around his neck and thanked him for saving her life, as well as all of the children that were as dead as she had been before the plane crash which was avoided by his action in moving the tanker.

With all `welcome backs` and `thank you'd` said, I made us all a pot of tea and Jane saw to Faiths needs before sitting down to listen to the message that Lindsey had been told to pass on and John also had something to tell us, from a dream he had the night before. Having seen him arrive unshaven and not at ease with himself or something else I enquired as to what was playing on his mind to which he said, "Ok I'll tell you and then you may feel as badly as I did over it"

Feeling his rough chin he said, "Remember how I said about knowing what would happen if we hadn't saved the child who has the destiny that we were told of. Well, I saw it and I cried for the things that humans greed for money and power will do to this planet and our home if this child fails in its foretold destiny."

"Well come on then, tell us what you saw" said Jane inquisitively. Continuing with his description John relayed his dream to us sniffing back a tear at what he had seen.

"I saw the Amazon rain forest burning so the ground could be built and grown on without a slightest thought or consideration being given to the effect on the world's climate, the wild life and environment or the lives of the native peoples that live there, and the ice caps melted causing many places to flood including London and a lot of New York " Taking a breath before carrying on with, "Another thing I saw was the way that the earth's crust was breaking up due to the countless companies mining for coal and minerals and drilling for oil. The mines and wells are starting to cave in making the surface sink. That is damaging the natural earth's surface causing more earthquakes and volcanic eruptions, killing millions on every continent. It has already started in small ways but it's being denied and the reason for it covered up by the big international companies and corrupt politicians who are getting rich from it"

He went on." At one point I saw an entire town in the United States sink into the ground as a new volcano erupted in the crater. It must have killed over a million people. Another thing I saw was an earthquake splitting California off from the rest of America; only it sank into the sea, killing countless people. That was because open casting had weakened the San Andria's fault, causing massive earthquakes. It's not too late yet and can be prevented as long as the child with the destiny to do so does."

Pausing for a breath before he continued with his tale he brushed his hand across his brow. "How many innocent people would have to die because of business greed for profit? The worse thing that I saw is what would happen here is on the ground next to the approach road into our town. I saw that a fracking operation had caused a small earthquake, leading to the earth splitting open and leaving a huge trench the entire length of the high street, bursting the gas and water mains and the buildings on either side of it to start falling into the trench on top of the traffic that had already fallen. I also saw one school bus covered by the front of the newsagents before any children could get out and clear of it. Thankfully I'll be long dead and buried before it could happen but it scares the hell out of me the level of destruction that we could cause and the amount of animals and plants that would become extinct because of us".

"What sort of world are we leaving to our descendants?" commented Jane looking either way to check our response's at what we had just heard. Now we all had the knowledge of what we all had to do during the years ahead, if we want our planet to survive as God intended it for us. Having seen a sneak preview of what future generation might have to face if nothing changes, I think we all felt a certain anger and sense of betrayal of every living thing on the planet, by those who worship profit and power above life and the beautiful planet on which we all live and depend on. I had never realised that if we continued treating the earth so badly we would not have anywhere else to go and live.

Realising that our baby Faith's own grand children would be affected by the possible horrific future I was so grateful that John had saved the child with the destiny to save us but at the same time felt sorry for the ones that would be killed needlessly beforehand. We will never be able to watch a natural disaster movie again without remembering what John told us that day with a tear in our eye. It strikes me as unbelievable the way that I had changed from being a non-believer only two years before, to someone who does not practise any religion but does not have the slightest doubt that God does exist and is watching over us at all times whoever and wherever we are.

Next it was Lindsey's turn to share what she had to say, so turning her gaze to Jane she started to speak. "When I was in the big room that felt like it was a waiting room before I was returned to life, I was talking to a man there who said that he was called Peter Maclean and had been murdered but is being blamed for stealing twelve million pounds from the bank where he worked and now his wife and children are suffering from threats and lies from others including his bosses and the national press. Can you find his body because a post-mortem will prove that he was murdered and was innocent so that his family can have closure over his death? He was quite a good looker as well."

Going on, she enquired, "I suppose it's a silly question, John, but do you have any idea about the man I just told you about?" "I may be wrong but it sounds like the case of the bank worker who stole a fortune and disappeared, we thought he had done a runner overseas. The police here, the euro police and even Interpol are investigating." was his reply to her.

"It looks like you are all wrong." I added getting intrigued by what we had just heard and wondering what we were hoped could do about it. The sound of Faith crying brought our get together to an abrupt end so John gave Lindsey a lift home before he went to work, I think with what we now knew fresh in his mind.

On the Saturday night Jane and I met both sets of parents, proudly showing off the dozen or so photographs taken of mother and baby during the short while since coming home. Jane's parents Russell and Debra and mine David and Marie were all mesmerised as they looked closely at every picture of their granddaughter. The most exuberant moment came when holding her hand in mine I knelt down on one knee and asked Jane to marry me which was unanimously welcomed and was answered by everyone with a "yes" and by my love with, "I will marry you" finishing off with a kiss.

During the following days until July tenth there was no news from John, Lindsey had travelled to Greece working, I was busy at work and Jane was enjoying being a new mother but that changed for us at 11.55pm when just like our previous experiences an image formed in our wall mirror showing a tied and gagged man being shot execution style in the back of the head followed by the words, "This is how I was killed on a farm in Suffolk close to a train track. There were six of them involved. Tell my family that I was not bad and I did not desert them like the press said I did." He also told us the date and time of it happening which would be helpful for us and then the image disappeared back to normal. We were both shocked by what we had just seen and felt very sorry for the affect that it must have had on the poor man's family.

It was the evening of the twelfth that we spoke to John again telling him about what we had seen in our mirror and after a short moment he said. "We know how Jane was able to come back and how we stopped the deaths at the air-show from happening I wonder if we can in some way prevent his murder and maybe prevent the crime from happening before the eclipse next month. Could a miracle happen again or will we have to settle for only a closure for his family?"

Speaking with John he found out that the crime in question was carried out on the day of the eclipse in 1999 time itself and the crime had been planned to coincide with it, the idea being to use the brief darkness during the eclipse to steal the money.

Rubbing her chin in thought Jane posed the question, "If we know what is going to happen and when can we make an anonymous call or even set a trap and catch the criminals in the act." I'm way ahead of you young lady and I'll deal with it tomorrow." answered John in his official policeman's voice quite pleased at her way of thinking. When Lindsey called the next day I had the pleasure of informing her of what was being set in motion by John and when we might be hearing about it on the news which pleased her immensely plus we would not need to do anything.

The next day the day of the eclipse Jane and I found that just like the previous time we were unable to witness natures gift of an eclipse because there was thick cloud coverage so we settled for sitting in front of the TV watching the reports from other areas and more importantly watching the news for anything about what John and his fellow officers were going to do regarding the big robbery. It wasn't until the national and international news came on the BBC channel at six pm that we heard the saddening news that during a police operation to capture a gang of robbers an officer had been shot while rescuing and the freeing of bank employee Peter Maclean.

Luckily he had not been seriously injured but was taken to hospital for treatment. Obviously, Jane had to call Lindsey and tell her what had just happened for which she thanked her asking us to deliver a bouquet of flowers to his bedside from her while he convalesced. In order to keep our knowledge of what was going down and how John claimed that he had heard it being planned by a couple of people that he was unable to see in a public bar.

So all in all during the space of two years we had witnessed the same eclipse twice, helped save over a hundred people from death after a plane crash, stopped a robbery and murder, Lindsey had almost died of cancer and been killed by an evil spirit before returning to life and most importantly, Jane had been returned to life after her being killed in an accident. With all of us we had discovered that sometimes God will use people to help others to do the right thing while in a way testing our own faith and trust in him and ourselves.

CHAPTER 8

By the first of September 1999 our lives had not only been given the 12 months between Jane's tragic death in an accident and an eclipse which brought her back to life and me, to live again and be blessed with the birth of our daughter Faith. Along with Jane's best friend Lindsey and our new good friend police detective John Ammet plus with the will of God we had prevented the deaths of over a hundred people including many young children after a plane accident at a show thanks to John's courageous action and saving the life of one child who's descendant was destined to save the planet from mankind's own actions and selfish greed. But all that was before the repeated eclipse.

"Now that everything has been done and we are all ok, can we go ahead and arrange our wedding my love?" asked Jane peering very seductively at me from our bed. "Yes of course sweetheart, let's do it quickly before Faith is christened." I replied. Reaching over to her right side to her bedside cupboard she picked up a notepad and pen to begin writing a list of things which we had to do before saying I do to each other, but the sound of our daughter needing her mummy or daddy to take care of her needs soon had us putting our plans on hold to get up and dressed. While Jane worked on her list of necessary things to do I took on the role of taking care of Faith by washing and dressing her before sitting down hand feeding her.

Joining us in the lounge Jane read out her list starting with asking John to be my best man and Faith's Godfather when we had her christened as well as Lindsey, we had to book some time off of work for our wedding and honeymoon, and of course the wedding itself, all jobs that we would be doing together except for the wedding dress that Lindsey would certainly be involved in. Everything felt almost like a fairy-tale for me but soon enough something happened to scupper our plans causing us both great anguish and worry.

It was on the night of the third Friday of the month that as we were about to turn off the lounge light before going to bed that we both felt a sudden chill pass through our bodies which we hadn't felt since our experiences during the previous year. Automatically we directed our eyes in the direction of the wall mirror where we had seen several dead spirits before including Jane's before her return to life.

We could have been knocked down by feather when the image forming before us was that of one of Jane's school friends called Penny Whitaker. "Oh Penny! What has happened to you?" she murmured seeing a good friend from school was now no more. Unlike the previous times neither of us experienced a movement to the scene of her demise showing us nothing that could help us to understand the circumstances surrounding what had happened to her at such a young age. "It was Wayne Brummet Jane he killed me because I was your friend and he wants revenge after you got him sent to that young offenders' place for trying to rape you. You and Mike are both in danger now. You got to stop him Jane." Wayne was the lad who I stopped from raping Jane before we fell in love and now had targeted her friend in his twisted sense of revenge on route to getting us.

That night we had to do a lot of serious thinking about what we were now facing. "Will we ever get a normal life without having to deal with others problems?" asked Jane as she lifted Faith up out of her cradle to cuddle like a child with their favourite dolly. Putting on as brave a face as I could under the circumstances I placed my arm around her waist and said, "Try not to let Wayne bother you my love, I'll go and have a talk with John and see what can be done about him." and then I placed Faith back down into her cradle before leading Jane over to our bed to hopefully sleep which she decided not to do as it was still only the morning.

After we had dressed, washed and eaten that morning I advised Jane to keep our door and windows shut and locked until I returned home because I had decided to visit John and tell him all about the night before. "Ok darling. When you see him why not tell him that we want him to be your best man and be Faith's Godfather." She called out as I walked out onto the road that led into the town.

My heart started to thump faster as I walked when I noticed the reflection of a slow moving car with blacked out windows tailing me. As I speeded up my walking rate the car suddenly increased its speed purposely coming straight at me before swerving not to hit me. Frightened out of my wits aware of Penny's message I turned around and ran as fast as I could back home again have scared for my love and our daughter.

When I rounded the last bend in the road back into the one where we lived I was greeted by the sight of the same car that had just swerved at me driving off from opposite our home making me even more concerned about Jane and Faith. Hurriedly rushing in through our front door I called out to Jane "Jane! Jane! are you both alright, has he got in to you?" "What are you going on about babe? We're both ok, why?" she answered telling me that Wayne had not managed to get into them which eased my worry temporarily, but made me determined not to leave them alone without me to protect them from any threat.

As I relayed to her what had just happened to me and what I had seen in the road outside she was obviously very disturbed saying, "We need to tell the police babe and let them get the bastard before anyone else is attacked or killed by him. Something seriously bad must have happened to him while locked up to turn him so bad." With that she had to call her best friend Lindsey and tell her all about what had happened during the last twenty-four hours making her very angry at Wayne and telling us that she was coming around to see us when she returned to the UK after finishing her current modelling job in Europe. "I can't feel sorry for him honey because he has killed Penny our friend." I said angrily afraid in response to her.

"I think that I should get on the phone and check up on her and find out what I can about for death." With that Jane went into our bedroom to get her address book, soon returning and calling the first of many people she knew to find out as much as she could. As we sat on our couch trying to reassure each other all of our uncertainty over what to do became clear to us when, a bullet came smashing through our lounge window crazing my arm before embedding itself into our wall.

Scared out of our wits I decided to firstly call John, briefly forgetting that after his shooting he would not be working but would almost certainly be at home with his wife and children. It was fortunate that I did because he straight away instructed me to keep all possible entrances to our flat locked and not too go out until he or fellow police officer's came to us. One hearing the shot and Janes scream one of our neighbours a retired nurse took us into her flat and dressed my bleeding arm as best she could with what she had handy while we waited for help to come.

It was only about five minutes later that from the road outside we could hear the sound of several police car sirens screeching to a halt outside and car doors being slammed shut. With his left arm up in a sling John called for an ambulance for me as he instructed his fellow officer's what to do while he came in and talked to us about Penny and Wayne after which he called his superiors to fill them in and get a search started for both of them. When the ambulance arrived I refused to go with them and leave Jane and Faith alone which John accepted on seeing my wound was not serious. It was not that long before the media vans started pulling up outside and the occupants of the other flats in the same building as us were escorted out to safety by armed officers through the rain to a place of safety.

By the morning the entire street had been cordoned off and a national man hunt had begun for Wayne after the body of penny had been found in the flat that she rented closer to the college where she had been studying to be a teacher of junior school aged children.

After three days of effort by the authorities with no luck a piece of good news came up by tracing his mobile phone use and signal to within ten miles of our location. Because the forensics people had discovered Penny's diary had mentioned that he intended to shoot us both and burn our bodies to get his revenge on us as well as he had shot penny through the head.

This time the news about Penny hit Jane very hard because there was no way that anyone could bring her back to life again. That did bother us both because if we hadn't talked in court he would almost certainly have avoided his incarceration after trying to rape her. What hurt Jane more was hearing that her friend had been raped and strangled by Wayne before shooting her which might have happened to her if not for my action preventing their earlier encounter at the youth club whilst at school? For me personally that was enough to justify my past action in interfering when something not right was happening to an innocent person.

It was only a matter hour after a crime watch report on the TV before Wayne was spotted by a member of the public sitting in his car outside of the store where I worked.

Because of the number of potential innocent victims if fire arms were used in such a public place the order was given to the army trained police sniper to shoot him to kill if he made any attempt to resist arrest. After trying to box him in with their squad cars in order to prevent his escape an officer ordered him to surrender. Unfortunately, Wayne raised a shot gun and fired in the direction of the police which triggering the single fatal shot by the police marksman killing him outright where he stood causing a sudden panic amongst the unaware public who had been busy with their own shopping but were now screaming in terror and rushing away from the scene for safety. Receiving the news of what had just happened and the realisation that we were no longer at risk of harm or even death from Wayne was understandably welcomed by us all, more so by Jane who straight away threw her arms around me kissing me ever so passionately.

With that finally over our own sleepy, small town was able to give a Hugh sigh of relief as everyone's lives were able to return to normal. Something that under normal circumstances would be welcomed by most, but for us after our talking with John unnerved us both. He informed us that although Wayne was now dead he had been able to make questionable friends while being punished for his attack on Jane and he could easily afford the cost of hiring another to be his bidding if wanted. With that he added that he had been looking into Wayne's finances and found out that only a week earlier he had paid out the sum of £10000 to an unknown party for an unknown reason.

As for us we were able to get on with our own lives such as the organising of our wedding starting with asking John to be my best man and taking on the role of Godfather to Faith. Jane had already asked Lindsey to be a Godmother and the next time that she saw her she intended to ask her to also act as chief bridesmaid. After speaking with the vicar of the very same church where Jane had been buried after her death, following an accident which now hadn't happened after the magic of the eclipse had brought her back to life, we booked our wedding to coincide with her grandparents wedding anniversary.

On the eighteenth day of March 2000 Jane dressed in her specially designed white wedding dress was walked by her proud father up the isle to where I was stood waiting with John by my side as best man to make our vows to each other before our guests and more impotently before God.

CHAPTER 9

It was as we were drinking our morning cup of tea whilst listening to the radio that the broadcast was interrupted with the news that a terrorist bomb had killed over a hundred innocent people at a public event in a European country with more than one hundred injured. Those responsible claimed that they were going to attack anywhere that did not follow their belief which was not most of the world. Governments and leaders all over world were united in their condemnation of this unforgivable act.

Placing our cups down Jane said "I wish that we could turn back the time and stop the evil bastards from ever doing what they have done." "Even saving one of the victims would be a small victory over the evil that is poisoning the minds and hearts of terrorist leaders. But for now let's try to put this out of our heads and go into town and do some shopping." It did not take much time for Jane to get herself and Faith ready to go and soon we were on our way.

Arriving at the town's main street I noticed a marked increase of police officers being seen by the public reassuring them that the threats made earlier by the terrorists had been noticed and were being taken seriously by the government. "Good morning you two and young Faith, how are you today came the sound of our friend John's voice." With the sparkle of happy motherhood on her face Jane replied with, "We're great thank you, but why is there more police out today. Is it because of what was on the news this morning? Do we need to be worried about it happening on the continent?" Cautiously John lowered his voice before informing us of his concerns. "You have heard nothing from me but unofficially higher up are very worried that we are going to be hit soon by the terrorists and can't stop them because all the suspected groups have denied any involvement in it plus a couple terror groups have offered any information they get. I suspect that even they are a bit scared that they will be blamed and attacked for whoever is responsible." He also told me that he was still aware of the potential threat to us paid for by Wayne Brummet before his death. We soon made our goodbyes and carried on with our shopping watching anything unusual around us unexpectedly sharing John's concerns.

We carried on with our shopping unaware of the solitary person who had been tailing us ever since leaving our home that morning. Walking back out of the clothing store were we had just been to buy Faith a new dress because she had grown out of her old one there was a bright flash followed by the sound of a gunshot and I slumped forward landing face down on the ground, I had been shot. A moment later I could see my own dead body just laid there with fresh blood coming out of my belly. Two young men who were nearby without the slightest hesitation threw themselves at the shooter knocking his gun from his hand and bringing him down. Jane who had screamed out in horror rushed forward to me as the general public who were there either stood stunned by what had just happened before them or gathered around to help in any way that they could.

As I watched my own now dead body a brilliant bright light appeared ahead of me and I could make out the figure of my deceased grandmother ready to welcome me to the afterlife but as I reached her everything changed. Gone was my grandmother and light and in its place stood a tall saintly looking man with his hand held up to stop me. "It is not your time yet, you still have a task to do, so return to your body and life and wait for your task that I have chosen you for." With that he vanished and I felt myself drawn back down into my body. The blood that was running out of my belly suddenly started flowing back into me and the bullet that had killed me just popped back out of me falling onto the ground in plain view of everybody there to their astonishment. I was still unconscious during this and Jane who was holding me so tightly and kissing my face still not aware that I was now not dead had to be helped by a lady who taken a hold of Faith's buggy helped her to regain her composure.

It was only a few minutes before an ambulance escorted by two police cars arrived to take over. Everybody were so thankful to the two courageous young men that had disarmed the shooter and held him down until the police could arrest him. Taking with them an ak47 weapon gun and taping off the scene for the forensics experts to do their work.

As for me the paramedics where just about to ask why I was apparently not dead or even injured despite the fresh blood stains on my shirt with a fresh bullet hole that had appeared in it but from out of nowhere John right on schedule turned up instructing them to take me to the hospital and wait for him to get there which they did as I was still unconscious.

While this was going on John firstly spoke with a hysterical Jane at seeing her new husband murdered before her advised her to go to me at the hospital, and then he turned his attention on to the two young men who were busy giving their official statements to the police after bravely bringing down and restraining the shooter of me before he could kill anyone else. The girlfriend of one of them had actually filmed the whole incident on her Mobil phone which would help the police to investigate and bring charges.

The next thing that I can remember is waking up in a small room surrounded by people in and out of police uniforms and Jane with her head rested upon my chest crying her sweet eyes out. John had told the hospital staff to place me into a private room with two armed police officers on guard. "Jane my darling, where am I, what's happened and why?" were the first words that I spoke once awake and seeing her crying.

On hearing my voice Jane lifted herself back to standing with a look of surprise and adulation that I hadn't seen since the birth of Faith before answering with, "We just saw you shot dead Mike you're alive again but how and why". "I know my love; I've been sent back to do something but I do not know yet" I told her unsure of almost everything. "I need to talk with John my love can you call him babe?" Even before I could finish talking John who was standing back from us said, "I'm right here with you my friend, what can I do." Still uncertain as to what lay ahead of us I firstly needed to know everything possible about any witnesses to what had happened and the guy who had appeared to have just murdered me.

John got onto his walkie talkie and asked whoever was at the other end to bring them to the hospital to help with his inquires and about 30 minutes later the door opened and an officer directed the two brave young men who had probably saved lives by their quick action. At first sight of me not dead as they seen laid out on the street but sat up and alive they both stepped back and looked at each other not believing what they were seeing before them.

"How is this possible?" stammered out one of them "You were shot; we saw it happen." "Errr you're right I was dead but now I'm back." I confirmed. Shocked both of the men had to sit down and steady themselves before another word could be spoken. At that moment the door was pushed open by an official pulling a mobile unit holding a TV and video player. "Sir please forgive my interruption but I think you need to see this."

Once connected to the mains he pushed play and we all watched as the recorded footage of earlier showed everything that happened. It began as the holder was recording her boyfriend and his mate sitting outside of the small cafe on our main street enjoying a hot drink and cigarette like Jane and I often did. "Look at the figure crouching down behind them taking something out of the sports bag he has, and note the clear blue sky with no clouds anywhere. Note the man has a dark shadow around him but nowhere else. I looked at Jane and she at me as if we both knew the cause of it.

The next thing to see was the man pulling out an AK47 gun and aiming it right at me and fired it. The woman holding her Mobil turned in our direction in time to catch me falling forward clutching my stomach before returning to her boyfriend and mate who without hesitation sprung to their feet and very quickly disarmed the unshaven, dark haired shooter and restrained him. When the girlfriend turned her phone back in our direction it plainly showed the bullet hole in my shirt and the blood that was flowing out of me, but it didn't end there as we all could see.

All around there was panic in the street with the screams of the pedestrians and screeching tyres of cars braking as it happened. As I lay there now dead around me there was a glow of brilliant white light and all the blood that had been flowing out of my wound started to go back into my body as the bullet that had just killed me fell out onto the pavement. John straight away looking directly at the two men and said, "Well gentlemen you have just seen exactly the same thing that we have and I am asking you to never tell anyone what you saw, not even your other halves any of this gets out it would create nothing but trouble. There must have a reason for this and I will work with Mike to discover it. If I have to do you mind my contacting, you?"

Once Jane and were alone again she asked me what actually happened during the brief time that I was dead as I believe that she knew inside that there was more to it than I had told. I placed my arm around her and recounted that I could remember about my experience. "The figure that sent you back to me would have been your guardian angel, he does what God tells him to do so God must need you for something important.

"Yeah" I said "But how are we going to explain away my miraculous recovery to everyone?". "I'll tell you what to say" came the voice from out of nowhere as the shape of I think my guardian angel slowly appeared in front of us with a strong smell of Lilac. "I have been sent to guide and help you to prevent the devil taking human souls by stopping the wrongs from being carried out in the first place. It is going to be a very hard and testing service that has been appointed to you so you had better get ready. Oh and you can call me Tabec" "One question I have to ask. That is how we can help people overseas." "There are already chosen people where needed." was the reply which helped us both.

After receiving an official discharge from the hospital we were met by a journalist looking for a story for his newspaper concerning my shooting. I was just about to try and excuse it away when as if by magic I felt the weight of something in my pocket which on taking it out revealed a pocket radio complete with a bullet lodged in it as reason for my being alive. After giving a quick story to satisfy the journalist we made our way to the safety and comfort of our home before calling John to have Faith brought back to us.

As everything turned out John managed to lose the film footage and put out the story that I was saved by my Walkman, which had stopped bullet and was able to return home again because the shooter had been caught and arrested by the police. This was enough to satisfy even the many witnesses who had actually been present.

For Jane, Faith and I we were just three people that were in the wrong place at the wrong time and soon enough all was forgotten about enabling us to get on with our lives. That is until Tabec interrupted our lunchtime meal with a mission.

Author's Gallery Over the Years

Figure 1. Home after first leg came off

Figure 2. Dressed up for Christmas 2011

Figure 3. Me in 2004

Figure 4. My Lovely Michelle 2007

Figure 5. Me with only one leg

Figure 6. My wife Michelle in 2003

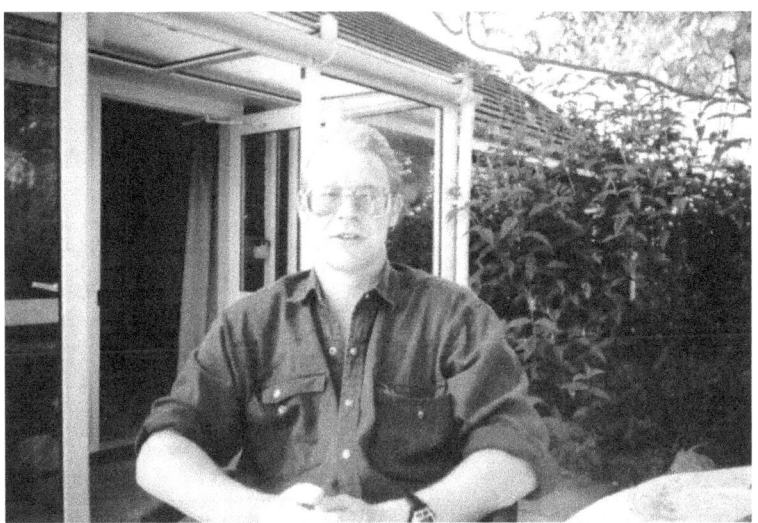

Figure 7. Me posing for picture

Figure 8. My custom-built Trike

Figure 9. Wedding day in April 2003

Figure 10. After 3 months using cannabis

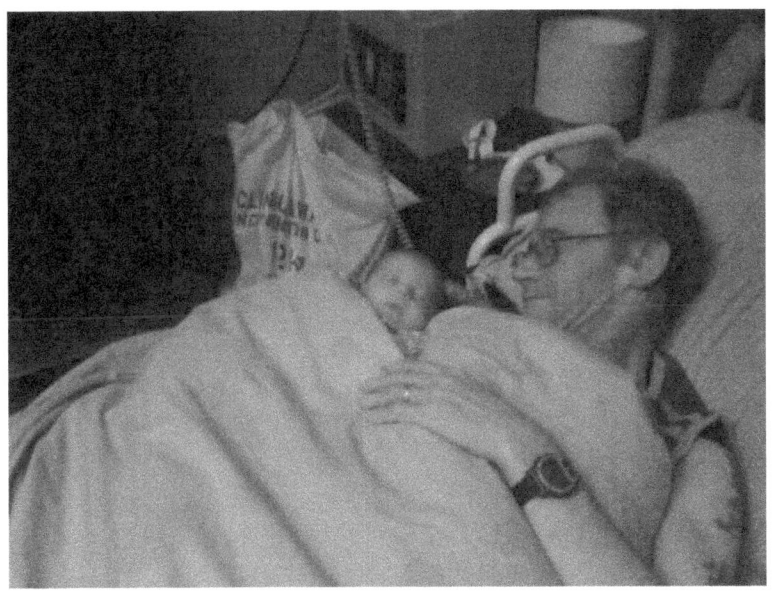

Figure 11. Granddaughter sleeps when grandad is there

Figure 12. Raising money for NABD national association of bikers with disabilities

Figure 13. After 4 months using cannabis

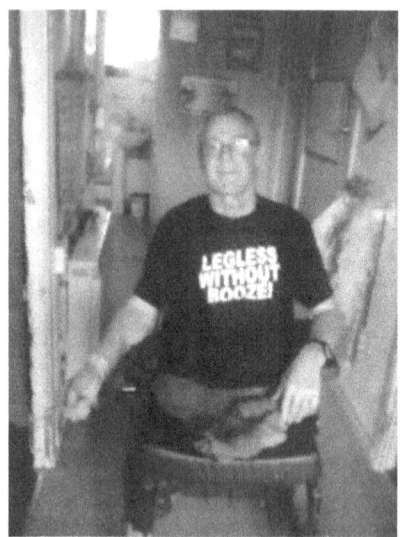

Figure 14. Me in Year 2012 with my Awesome T-shirt Sign

www.ingramcontent.com/pod-product-compliance
Lightning Source LLC
LaVergne TN
LVHW020431080526
838202LV00055B/5127